I0782149

KING KONG

KING KONG

IAN BLOOM

Natural

IAN BLOOM

Ian Bloom is an American art dealer and founder of Natural Gallery.

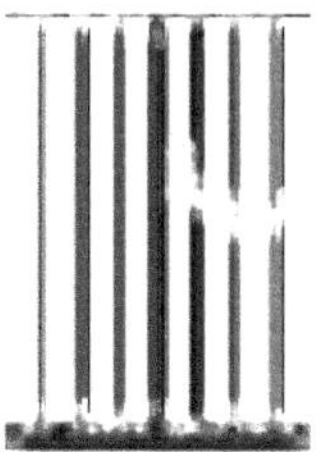

King Kong

I

THE DEVIL KILLED HER TODAY. No one believes me, but I know. I don't know how. But I know. I got a phone call from the past: "She's dead. Funeral next week. Top secret." I wish I cared more. I only think about myself.

Did I call the Devil forth? Whose will? Where is God? I knew God liked me. In the dark, I play the hero. But maybe it wasn't just God. The devil is the hero. And he liked me because he saw him in me. God is omnipotent. The hero rebels. The devil is the hero.

But he killed her today. He let her die. He took her away. Or was it God?

It was on a road lined by trees parallel to the mountain pass beneath the museum, about fifteen miles from downtown. I rented a luxury vehicle and drove from the airport to the site. The comfort of the shell and power of the engine kept control. It was sealed off like an art exhibit. Bent metal creased into the rock. My return flight was tomorrow.

The boss let met go but he wanted me back in the office. We had a deadline. He couldn't refuse me with an excuse like that. I had said, "I have no choice." He stared blank beyond. The silence made me question what I had said. What purpose did it serve? It was apparent and I owed him nothing. He should have offered more time and shown heart. But he'd probably reflect and come strong with sympathy upon my return. For now, it seemed fake. She wasn't dead. After the funeral, it'd be final and the absolute closes the door.

I drove to Getty Oil. The sky burned free of clouds. I ate at the café by the market. They recognized me but no one knew why I was back. No one cared because no one knew and I didn't tell them. I remembered what she told me, "No one loves you like I do." When I walked to the door, I pulled and it locked, so then I pushed and got out. My mind was elsewhere. The route through the canyon rising to the mountains was windy and I'd borrow a shirt and tie from Marcel. His uncle had just died.

I sped through the warning light at the museum intersection. Instinct pushed life into my hand on the wheel. He wasn't home. In the shade, at the apex, the sun glared. Perhaps it was the flight, the drive, and the general rush that I didn't expect to be here, that compelled me to sleep. The shade covered the hood and then the pavement, so I woke wanting a smoke and a shower. A smile through the window offering me both. I said, "Yes," and he saw I was the way I was so he tossed the key through the gap and let me be.

The driveway was long and windy, too. It was locked but he had left. The key gave me control. I didn't want to see her, but I saw her in a photograph. It was us three, at that moment before it went a different way. When he got back, I was fresh and was right to talk. He was busy, on the phone, so I waited. The ocean was visible like a temptation to imagine, too far to cool. Off the phone, he poured and handed and we drank in unison. He was grand and virulent and the energy envisaged strength for me. We shook hands and smiled the way history makes it real. He had all the knowledge, stating, "She died instant. No pain. I know you loved her, so you should be here." I thought it was a slight on my red shield but my apathy sought connection. I felt weak for the desire to explain. But he kept at it and let me maintain. "It is what it is, or, rather, what it was. It's obvious and it's a big deal, but you let it go. You didn't want the hassle. Timing. She needed a budget. Your earnings were volatile. And if truth is a bullet, she didn't have a dream." I said, "I had a dream of her dream." He backed, "Yet, she had comfort here, steady soma. She didn't need to look and kept thought sedated in routine. You're young at heart, an ideal romantic, and it must have been hard for the both of you."

Stark stance. Silent, agreed. When she was with me, it was

ten years gone, and when it wasn't, she used to pass the moments together spectating with her eyes, glad for my presence. For the moments in between the silence, she slept, exercised, and stayed on the level. But that was because she was a rock, and I was fire. A flickering candle in the light, beaming up and down, for the banter of entropy. A few months later and she would have stayed the same. A dormant heart, incapable of expressing the eruption. That's more than less why I suppose I let myself forget, at least for a while. And also because the birth of tragedy was preferable to avoid. I wanted to feel something, even if it wouldn't last. And if memory cast her in haze, three years and no words. I moved to the other city, and then the other city across the ocean, and so far ahead in zoned time that she was always in the past, and I could go back, when I was ready, because I was ahead. But I was wrong. And really, the distance kept it easy, so I could avoid packing, buying airfare, and spending twelve hours traveling.

Marcel lit two cigarettes and handed me the first. Silent but visual interplay. A morphology of conscious gravity. Broken by speech. He said, "I suppose you want to see her again." I looked him in the eyes and he carved a path to the drawing room. Through the foyer, he detailed, "I was at this masquerade and she was there, and the photographer, of course, and yeah, you'd appreciate. The real life. A smile. Whenever there's one of these parties, after the big award show, or the premiere of a real hit, there's always suspense, because lives are made public and things change." We went to the terrace and the smokes were halfway. There were fast cars against the blind canyon raids like the sounds of crashing waves. As we stood, the engines volumed up and down. And then we'd start, and the engines would resound closer and closer. The sound was like a shocked heart. Marcel crushed the cigarette and handed me a photo album. "I'll be in the studio, fine sir Reuter. If you need, don't knock. Tonight, there's a party, the funeral's tomorrow at ten. There's a lot going on, so in your place, I'd cancel that flight and extend your stay. One more thing: she wrote you a letter but you can't get it until tonight, and I've taken the power to arrange for you to get it at the party. I wanted to let you know, before you say no." I nodded thanks. She was never a writer.

I looked in. The visage that ran the infinite war. I analyzed the setting. Her eyes. Yeah. An innocent Eve floating in a banal manicured paradise. It was a very bright, raw blood room with ornamentation and catharsis. The furniture was staged Beaux-Arts and some Le Corbusier seats to enact a tilt. Two of the Le Corbusiers, in the middle of the room, were empty, like thrones, and an altar table, like a captain's door, ready for human sacrifice. The sun shaped hue of light reflected from the chandelier. Near the table was an Egyptian obelisk, a Masonic All-Seeing Eye, and a replica of Donatello's David. I wanted simple. But I had Versailles.

Just then Marcel returned behind me. He must have been eager. He composed. "Change of plans. It's right now. I'm supposed to pick up this model with a PhD in Art History, her friend's in town from Milan, perfect for you, but they're already there. I'm supposed to take them with us so we get a better parking spot for the getaway." He was choosing which car to take, with the keys in a binder. He said, "You want to drive?" I answered, "No." He was nonplussed, and I felt false for having said that. He looked me in the eye and directed, "Why would you not?" but without tension, as if he just failed to understand. I said, "Timing." He scratched behind his right ear, and then, went back to the keys.

When the clock struck seven, Marcel said, "The Range Rover. For the way back. Shotgun's waiting for you." I'm not certain how I showed face, but he stayed there a moment where he was, to the side of me. Having this support system piercing my soul was not comforting. The room beamed with the casting western light. A hawk perched on the terrace rail. I could sense I preferred a nap. Without eye contact, I said to Marcel, "You can go ahead." Chainsaw reaction he answered, "Like hell. I want to play you my new album"—as if he'd been designing the plan around this point.

After the engine firepowered and the doors locked, he kept quiet. He would have been very confused if anyone had told him he would end up caring what an accountant had to say about his art. He was thirty-six and came from Hollywood. At the point after the hit single guitar solo, I interrupted the sound. "Oh, you're ready for mastering." Then I remembered that before taking me to the studio before the recording sessions, he had talked to me about Freya. He'd told me that she was engaged to a builder, and they were wedding soon, given the timing. When a boxer plays up in weight class, it's all about speed. That was when he told me her sister confided she had second thoughts and that Marcel had found it hard to process. In Hollywood they keep the narrative dramatic, especially for an engagement. But after plans are set as all weddings, you barely have time to get used to the idea before you have to start running after the train. Then her sister had said to him, "I don't think she's in love with him." Marcel apologized yet stated it's a fact. I stepped in and said, "I disappeared." I thought what he'd been saying was inevitable and made sense.

In the wide driveway he read my mind and brought it up because he was concerned. He had solid success and prospects ahead, so he'd offered to take on the job of big brother. I pointed out that even so he was still too busy on location and on tour. He said no, he wasn't. I'd already been struck by the way he had of saying "love" and "hope" and, less often, "the wedding," talking about her, when some of the parties involved weren't our friends. But of course it was about rank. He was the movie star, and to a certain extent he had a top down view.

Just then the models spotted us. Black night shaded fast. Deep clouds out of nowhere through the skylight. The same house as the photo. The red curtain and the black night in the foyer. I was blinded by the overload of Christmas style light. Marcel suggested I go to the center for the buffet. But I didn't want food. Then he proposed he concoct potent cocktails with spice. I like bitters and rocks, so I agreed, and he returned a few minutes later with iced gasoline. I drank automatic. Then it was right to smoke. But I stopped, because I thought what if I ran into one of her friends, how it would look, even though she was dead. I replayed the thought; it was futile. I offered Marcel one of mine and we smoked.

At one point he said, "You are aware, her friends will be here. It's obvious. I have to go entertain for the ride back, I really like her." I told him don't leave me alone but I didn't mean it. The partygoer chaos was making me dizzy. He said he'd never. That was how he operated: it was all out in the open but it was always arms-length. He left, brought them back, freed some seats. On a pedestal in the middle he arranged our drinks like pieces on a chessboard. Then he sat down direct from me, the models on both our sides. Her friends saw me from the west side of the grounds. I didn't look at them. But the way they looked my way made me think they were talking about me. It was a relief; the drink granted me a lightweight buzz, and the smell of roses through the trickle of smoke and grilled meats came through the open door. I think I meditated for five minutes.

It was a question from the angel model to my left that put me back in place. Because I had that thousand yard stare, the sheer velocity of focus on her seemed sharp and vibrant. There wasn't a blemish of humanity on her face, and every texture, every angle and no makeup reinforced she was perfect that it made my insides twist. That's when her friends approached. There were five in all, and they blocked out the firepit so they were framed by light. They brought chairs. It was a moment and I noticed every detail of their looks and their ornamentation. But I didn't want to listen to them, and it seemed a dream with ghosts, dead alive. Almost all of her friends had leather jackets, and the zippers, which were zipped up, bound their waists like corsets, making their breasts project bold and proportionate. I'd never noticed how leather made a woman's body enflamed like natural armor. Almost all the men passing by looked our way and drank Coronas. What I observed most was that I wasn't able to see their reactions, just a subtle turn from the corners of the eyes. When they'd gone out of range, most of them stood their ground and nodded at Marcel, I suppose, since he kept the chin going up and down and the hand waving back and forth, so that I couldn't tell if they were friends or acquaintances. I think they knew me too but with my back turned, there were no greetings. It was then that I connected they were positioned like spectators in an amphitheater, behind me, basking in the atmosphere, grouped around Marcel, center stage. For an instant I had the absurd notion that they were there to tear me apart.

Soon one of her friends started crying. She was next to Marcel and I knew her too. She gathered her composure, the beating heart slowing down. I wanted her to stop. The others seemed to let it be. They sat there, in the extended circle, smoking silent. They looked at me and I looked at them and the models didn't know what was going on. We didn't fill them in. Marcel kept up the entertainment. It didn't surprise me, because I knew how he was. The moment seemed to spoil but I had no compulsion to say a thing. Marcel leaned over and said something to his lust interest, and she smiled, shook her head in comedy, whispered something in his ear, and ran off. Then he switched seats so he was beside me. After a long smoke pull he explained, "She gets nervous with death. She knew her too in passing. She says that she was the only girl that didn't judge her in acting class and now she's alone."

Us and her friends sat there smoking silent for what seemed too long. As Marcel had switched seats, the crying friend had calmed down. She wiped her mascara and peered at her eyes through her lipstick mirror. Thank God she shut up. I wasn't dizzy anymore, but I didn't want to say anything to her friends and the seat was uncomfortable. I was waiting for them to make a move and confront me on reality but they didn't, and this started to annoy me. Except twice, first immediately when I looked at them right and left, and then twice when I put a cigarette between my lips and then struck flame I saw their mouths open with no words. Finally they got out their mobile telephones and faced down like pious worshipers. They were so lost that they acted like they didn't care that we were all there for death, that it didn't matter. But I think back and that was just me being uncomfortable in the chair.

A waiter came by with cookies and coffee. We all ate and sitting with each other was comforting, even though the chair wasn't. It would not be proper to get up and leave. The party went on. I recall using eye drops at one point and seeing that I looked sad, her best friend gave me the letter in a sealed envelope. Her handwriting, my name. Another friend I never really talked to but always said hi to through history looked grave and beautiful when she stared at the handoff. Then I displaced, pocketed it, and put on the thousand yard stare once more. I came to with a tap on the shoulder. Fireworks were coming. Soon thereafter, one of the friends lit a joint and coughed unnatural. She turned away to cover the tension, because coughing is not becoming to anyone. She passed it around, and Marcel told them to give it to me. Her other best friend looked at me honest and smiled with charm. I finished the joint and got up. So did they. The muted symposium had left us dank in scent and pensive in mood. We all hugged before we carried on with pretense. Her best friend held my hand—as if that night during which we hadn't had a conversation had in a real sense made us closer than ever.

I was high again, rare and beyond tolerance. Marcel showed me the house and I washed my face in a luxury bathroom. I recalibrated with bottled water and more cookies, which settled my state. I napped for twenty minutes on a couch. When I went outside, there were no more fireworks. Above the hills that separate the valley from the city center, the streetlights are brighter because there is more darkness on the road. And the cool breeze rising over the hills brought the smell of dried flora on pace to burn. It was going to be a dry winter's day for night. It had been a long time since I'd been up this road, and I desired to walk random even though she was dead.

So I waited by the fountain above the driveway, by a wall covered in bougainvillea. I concentrated on the constant water running and I wasn't high anymore. I considered time space and where I'd be elsewhere. The office was in the future and my colleagues would be heading in now. That was always when the nature of the day struck me. I'd wake and my decisions were made. I envisioned the routine a bit more before focusing on an insider conversation about stocks and drugs on the other side of the wall. There was some hushing and then nothing. The full moon glazed through the disintegrating clouds deep in the sky. A cool breeze shuddered my spine. Marcel came out and said they're looking for me. I had no choice and so I went. Her best friend made me read the letter. I noticed her leather jacket was unzipped and she had been working out. She picked up her mobile phone and looked at me. "Do you want to see her? The mortician said she's nice. Her mother is having it closed casket so this is your only chance. It's up to you." I said no. She said she'd call back: "Never mind."

Then she told me she can pick me up for the procession and I thanked her. She sat down next to me on the bench and crossed her long legs. She pointed out that she wanted me to sit beside her during the funeral, not her friends. Everyone was supposed to be there. After there'd be a celebration of life. "It's more suitable," she defended. But in any case her widow—the builder—was hosting. At that she smiled serious. She said, "It makes sense. They had a happy marriage on the surface. We used to tease her and say, 'Estate queen.' She'd laugh. They all had fun. And the truth is he's devastated about Sigrid's death. I offered help but he wanted none. But on the advice of my girlfriends, I didn't invite him tonight."

We just sat there for a while. She stood up and looked out the window to the yard. Suddenly she said, "She still thought about you. You were too late." She warned me that this would happen. Not the dying part, but the losing her. She cracked the window. I got up and sat on the sill next to her. We smoked. She said it would be longer than expected because there were a lot of speakers at the church. We went back to the party space. Center front of the yard stood Marcel and the two models. The one he liked was holding a bottle of champagne, and Marcel put his arm around her shoulders, rotating a strand of her hair. As we approached, Marcel let go and stood straight up. He cherished me "hominis" and said a few sacred words in jest. He said I should drive and started to the car; we followed.

The road was dark but I wasn't high. The models laughed and the handling was impressive. When we got back, the champagne bottle in hand, they went to have fun. I sat with her friend and her personality was subtle. She waited for me to do something. We didn't drink but we smoked. She was still waiting, expecting. I wasn't sure of myself. But then I looked at her again, and she smiled. I decided to play the role, smiled back, and we went, too. She made me feel good because I made her feel good. It was honest. It felt pure. In another context, I'd sit across a table from her and eat happy. But the right timing was just this once. When we were done, I fell asleep.

At the church, the Cadillac hearse arrived and the casket looked like a portal to the underworld. It was wood but it shone like a death metal guitar case in the gray sunlight. The carriers were the builder, her brother, her father, and someone I didn't recognize. I could hear the metronome of chatter condense as the casket directed attention inside. It was over before I could pay attention. I went to the bathroom and stood in front of the mirror for most of the time. I smoked outside with a brother. Then it was over and they were all coming out. Marcel found me, "Mr. Reuter." He introduced me to two attendees. I didn't register their names; I just recognized that they were attorneys from her firm and that they were single. Without pretense the taller one lowered her severe, soft face. Then we stepped down to the right to clear a path for the body. We followed the carriers and left the church. On the road, the hearse engine was loud. Detailed, luscious, and intimidating as a shark, it looked like the President's limo. At the passenger door was the mortician, a fat man in an expensive suit, and a skinny average man. I realized that it was the builder. He had a Constantin Vacheron watch and Brunello Cucinelli shoes, a Tom Ford suit, and a black tie too skinny for the occasion. He was barely keeping it together. His eyes were all pupils, his pallor was blood deficient, and his hands showed too many veins on pulse. His hair had no style, like a buzzcut overgrown, and I wasn't impressed. She was already loaded in the back. We got in our vehicles and I watched them bury her on the mountain.

The sunlight baked sweat under my suit. The tension warmed rising. I looked away as they lowered her. This was the first funeral I'd seen with a majority of youth. It seemed unnatural. The tall attorney was in talking distance. She mentioned that they would go for walks on their lunch breaks throughout the city center and on a particular building overlook, especially in the late afternoon when the sun left the office landscape to the shade. Maybe I was hopeless too soon. An evening walk implied reflection. Reflection assumed dreams. Was it about me? I was the strongest personification of what if, for her, that, I knew. A kind of black comedy fantasy, too filled with horror and ecstasy to take with action. But the attorney's description emphasized the contrast. It was baking and the mountain was heating, absorbing its tan, shameless and committed.

Thank God it was over. I noticed a lot of cigarette smoke on the way to the vehicles. Marcel drove so I paid attention to the sights. The sun was peaking and the sunglasses cast the roads in a rose tint. We had the air conditioning on full power but cracked the windows open for another cigarette. The sound of wind clashed with the heat battling the cool air. I wiped my brow with a handkerchief. Marcel said, "Pretty hot." I said, "Typical." He revealed, "I'm glad to get out of there." I said back, "Everyone knows who you are. You belong." A pause, a real sigh, and a finality, he explained, "You're the lost love. You're safe in the mystery." This cryptic tag numbed my face and I threw the cigarette out of the window and shut it up. The road was open and Marcel increased the speed. The attorneys were following us. I looked through the mirror and then at Marcel. Hounds. No wasted action.

We hit some traffic at the freeway entrance. He didn't pass so the attorneys could drive relaxed. The car felt too cold now but the sun provided a greater evil. The glare was blinding even with the rose tint. We passed the sight of the crash and didn't mention it. The bent metal scarred into the rock and glistened in the sun. The pavement was new on the next bend of road hugging the mountain pass and the tires were quiet. I knew I was a little lost in the finality of the procession and the anonymity of being physically present but mindfully shrouded. The gray and white sky and the mahogany red of the car hood seemed to reinforce the carnal brutality of decay, indifferent to life. We were in a fueled casket and it was all a matter of time. The dried black of the asphalt, the matte black of our suits, the shiny black of the leather interior, and the blood red of the metal shield. All the colors, and the sweat, the cigarette smoke, the A minor Beethoven symphony, made my head focus harder to stay grounded. I was fighting the mental tide, from getting high the night before. We went right over the freeway, and the builder was behind. By the university, we lost him to a long bend in the road uphill. It was a green light and he overtook us at full speed. Timing. The attorneys decided to play a game and Marcel let them win. We went into the slalom and they knew where we were going. I felt the blood flow pressuring my veins.

We pulled up and parked for a quick exit. I didn't have to meet him, but I shook his hand anyway, because I was on his property. He didn't care. He didn't know who I was, and even if he did, it was better for the both of us that we didn't take it anywhere. I forgot the whole thing, except that, and a remark from the other best friend. She wasn't at the party the night before but her black dress made a scene in any setting. Her voice had the allure of intellect for an opera singer, not a swimsuit model. The inflection and cadence incited pleasure, in spite of my apathy. She said, "Well, there were no kids, so you really never had anything to worry about. You went too fast

without her, and if she was going too slow, you didn't want to wait."
It was plain and valid. I controlled my emotions and actions. I lived
with the consequences. No escape. Snapshot images from the wake
crackle in my mind, as polaroids overexposed. A rotting camera ob-
scura. The builder, alone, against the view of sky and city. Silent tears
on his face. I almost felt bad for him. But what I really thought of
him was repulsion. Just to get away from me. But this made no sense
because I was in his space and his scenario. He didn't wipe the tears.
They dried on his face until he had to when a friend approached. I
broke observation. Also, the girlfriends circled together in a séance of
smoke by the gazebo, the ivy vines slithering about their collarbones
as a crown of thorns for the collective medusa. A unified sorrow. The
newly curated roses at the center of the table, the spilled vodka expanding the grass contours, the sound of a truck engine, a motorcycle
ignition, another fountain with larger pipes, and my authentic smile
of leisure upon departure and crossing the tunnel from the mountains
to the valley that was Los Angeles and I knew I was free to do as I
please and sleep without dreams.

II

AS I CAME TO, I thought of the timing. My boss wasn't happy, and, he had a right. Yet, these events are beyond an office commitment. So, I had no remorse. Now, I was prepared to take off a whole week. Let it all burn. Today was Monday, but it felt like Sunday, because I had flown back in time Saturday and the present never seemed to catch back up. I was out of time, ahead, Tokyo, Zürich, back to a Los Angeles frozen capsule. At the core, her death was beyond my control, and though she was already buried, I was entitled to processing time. I could gauge my boss's perspective but I didn't care to exert effort.

I laid there, foot out the sheet, not quite rested essential. I suppose the day before was heavy and it had an effect. In the mirror, grooming, teeth brushing, washing away the heaviness, I decided I'd drive Sunset Boulevard to the beach highway and go to the county line. The tall attorney was still asleep but she had given me her card the previous night, so, that was that. I took the Porsche because it was my favorite engine and I didn't want to drive manual transmission. I hit 100 before Amalfi Drive and an old man in a Rolls Royce blared his horn at me. What a fool. Sunset Boulevard with no traffic is a no man's land. Speed tempts death at every curve, especially beyond the freeway. He should know better. At the county line, I descended the stairs entombed by the rocks and waded into the water until I could submerge my head. It wasn't crowded. A tall beauty having swimsuit photographs with a small crew, a Mediterranean man and Germanic woman together, and a group of Japanese tourists. When I finished and got to the car, the tall beauty was at her car and the camera crew was gone. We smiled at each other and I didn't turn on my phone because I knew Marcel and the tall attorney would follow up. She asked me what I thought and I said it looked okay. She was new to town and seemed practical with goals, not dreams. She hit the marks with her physique. I'm only 5'9" so when a woman is 5'11" and built, I know she has pace, strength, and perspective. She saw my body, so I hit her marks with my physique, too, I think. But we exchanged contact information and she drove off fast and sharp. That turnout made her even more desirable. I had helped her with directions and when we hugged, her breasts expanded on my heart. It was nice, and intimate, considering we had just met. A man is a man and a man's thoughts naturally sexualize in an innocent way. I played my notes with precision and we were comfortable without shoes and clothes, so we planned a date before I left for Tokyo. She laughed when I stopped my words mid sentence to stare the horizon and disclose my plans. It was that moment I decided the week off was defined, and I'd fly to Tokyo before returning to the office. An inevitable sequence of events, and she was top rank. She said, "I'm still so white." I said, "You're not burning, you're glowing." Then I asked to see her later under the moonlight with some Mexican food or a movie. She said she'd never been to Casa Vega and that Wim Wenders' *Wings of Desire* was playing at an independent theater. She knew of it as *Der Himmel über Berlin*, or Heaven above Berlin in English, and wanted to see it because she hadn't in her home country because she was from a small town by Weimar, not a metropolis like Frankfurt. She asked why I was visiting and I had to say I was here for a funeral because I didn't want to lie to her. She asked who. I did the long stare to the horizon again and then said this girl who was in love with me but had married someone else. She stayed composed with a smile, asked how long ago, so I said, "Three days ago." She did a stare of her own and then looked in silence. I chose not to give her the details, but I did want to because she seemed resilient. We both looked off and then back towards each other and she asked if I still loved her. I said, "No, she's dead." And then, she said, "Yes, tonight at 6:30, the show starts at 9:00." We weren't cold. Life is a brutal scam. You love the memory because death eliminates the continuity. The movie's over.

And you forget about it. It's meaningless. I don't want to change. I can take the guilt but kill the love.

I drive fast down the coast, so I took my time. I let her go ten minutes ahead because I didn't want to catch up to her. I spotted her at the curve past the fire station and then at the hill by the university, so I refueled at the town center gas station to lose her with certainty. After a smoke, shower, second nap, and salad, I picked her up in the Lexus LX. The food delivered and the energy of the patrons catalyzed our connection. I admit I was having a good time. I barely had the chips and guacamole, and I didn't finish my tacos. She had a margarita on the rocks, and I told her how that there are consequences to learning how to act. I warned her but didn't want to go in detail because she was set on studying the Stanislavsky method. It was distinct that I had more to say but she put it off to build suspense. At the theater, we paid attention to the movie but she put the arm rest up in between us, so we could touch legs. Her elbow hit my abdomen and her hand rested on my leg. She claimed ownership, and that made her more attractive. Toward the end of the picture, I wanted to kiss her, but I held out. Then, when there was a profound insight to the human condition by the angel in the movie, she gripped my leg with her hand. I had my arm around her hip. I squeezed. She squeezed, too. Then I kissed her fast, but it wasn't strong. I started to drive her home but Marcel's was closer, so she came back.

When I woke, she acted asleep, so I could wake her up. We did it once, I had a smoke on the terrace, and she kissed me goodbye, "See you soon." It was Tuesday and now I had to inform the boss of my plans. He knew my general attitude, yet even with assumption, the decent gesture would be to tell him plain. I did that quick and fast, and he had no real answer because I was free to do as I pleased. I was already 6,000 miles away. Even in the case he held it against me in the future, I was the American and I had knowledge he couldn't replace. I fast rid my mind of the situation and thought of Freya. I was referring to her by name because I suppose I liked her, in my own possible way. I laid there in bed and actually replayed the scenario, from the beach to the parking lot, then to the highway, the restaurant, the theatre, and now here. She had to pick up her university friend from the airport. I noted a strand of her long blonde hair between the pillow and sheet. I took my mobile phone with her pillow between my arms as support and could smell what scent she had left. I slept some more and stared at the ceiling, the mobile phone screen, the silence. I didn't want to go out for lunch because it still felt like Sunday. Every morning so far felt like a Sunday one because of the Saturday night feeling from the activities in the dark. Marcel asked me with raised brows equally curious and concerned. I was outdoing him because that's how he interpreted it. There is no competition but he had no other way to ground his perspective. He started and stopped with the spinach and eggs and wooed me with a Knusper sandwich because she was German.

After lunch there was an interlude, my stomach had more blood than my mind, and she got back on my mind. Valeria, not Freya. I said her name out loud under my breath and on impulse went outside and smoked resolve. A weak defense mechanism. I thought of us, in my forest cottage off Wonderland Avenue, when I was young and stupid, and how the statue on Marcel's coffee table had traversed both environs, symbolized the connection. Me and her sitting on that couch, a perfect size, dare I admit, real potential for a home. But she never dreamed. And my dream of her dream coming to life died. When I decided to go, I got rid of that place because it was too big and having her there had ruined it for when she wouldn't be. I only kept my Joe Colombo Elda chair and a framed photograph of the Getty Museum that my father had taken inverted with the travertine stone columns and the ceiling by the café. Marcel got the statue, a replica of Rodin's Le Penseur. It was too serious. That position garners strain, tension, not ease. It's subtle but there's clear effort. The cigarette finished its purpose and I was back to the present, overlooking the mountain range to the clouds and the ocean.

I picked up a Wall Street Journal newspaper but dropped it for the weekend magazine. I liked the advertisements. Sometimes I would sit with a model and she'd keep me company while I ate alone. I tore out an ad for an Italian designer because she was flawless and the interior colors composed a pleasant dichotomy of space and softness. When commercial ads caught my eye, I'd collect them in a binder for reference for my paintings, whether they be Titian style portraits or De Kooning inspired car crashes. I washed my face, and then took a book on the history of the Habsburg empire to the terrace.

The terrace from the guest room looked out on the same view as the living room, high west to the mountains and to the sea. The canyon road zig zagged across the rock with natural suspense. Yet it had been a misty morning so the road seemed darker with the water. The sounds of tires was muted thus, and the few cars were exotic and fast despite the slip of the road. A legion of bicyclists jutted out from a blind curve and a Lamborghini had to wait its turn. The bicyclists in caution yellow garb resembled a banana as they slalomed in sequence. The Lamborghini engine purred light and then grappled loud upon overtaking the bicyclists. My eyes followed the Lamborghini to an overlook where a couple was smoking and then kissing beside a convertible classic Ford Mustang. This was a nondescript residential road, free of the tourist crowd, so the pause on the road seemed more monumental given its isolation. Perhaps they were distinguished in the area or had by chance taken the road as guests to a proprietor up the way. The sun cracked open and I could see leather reflecting against their bodies in grasp. This added to the iconography. Then they got in the convertible and made a U turn out to the city. I considered their future path, perhaps to the cinema, to a café, the beach, or maybe just a pleasant nap on the calm Los Angeles afternoon.

After they disappeared west, there was no action. The empty street receded into the mountains without catalyst. I didn't want to do any active thinking so I readied myself for a casual drink and smoke with my book at the café by the market. Instantaneous viewing grounds for pretty women and random characters. There were some distinguished retirees and young Hollywood hustlers on the social make in the booths and some existentially bent loners at the counter. The sun cascaded split slit through the blinds like a noir film shot colored chiaroscuro. I sat outside so I could smoke. They let it go here even though Los Angeles was not friendly to the act in public space. A dapper Spaniard trio did the same to my right, and a quiet American with a French girl did the same to my left. Across the street the art gallerist set a chair outside so he could do the same. He wore a burgundy smoking jacket and had no socks on between his driving shoes and loafers. He crossed his legs so his ankles shown in focus prominent and at a hard contrast to the black slacks. A group of Ivy League university types departed in a parent's vehicle and a loud woman on a mobile phone cleared out some shopping bags into a Mercedes G class wagon so the street was empty. Two athletic women with greyhounds walked side by side and there it was, the post high noon desert of the real on an outpost road. My mind wandered to John Ford and the tension of an event on the precipice of piercing the silence. Had Liberty Valance made an entrance and a shootout occurred, I picture framed the angles and the music, crossing with a Sergio Leone Ennio Morricone mix of grandeur and crescendo. At the café next to the gallery, the fine moustache and greased hair proprietor swept aggressive the cigarettes butts and leaves to the street. I noted the large alcohol license sign in his window and like clockwork entered some tailored suits without ties to unite form and content. A Tuesday before the schoolkids would get out and the office workers would unleash the traffic hoard. But these guarantees did little to breach the sedate pulse of the outpost road.

I shifted my chair and angled it so my right elbow could rest on the back the way the art gallerist had positioned his seat across the road. Mirror images, smoke, trail, and gaze. I felt comfortable like this for a few cigarettes before I ordered a lemonade and reverted to typical posture. I looked at a pretty woman with huge square sunglasses enter and exit my viewing plane with a Napoleon cake and decided to eat one, too. Outside, I consumed and crunched the creams into pure fulfillment with the cigarette as a balanced dessert. The clock above the independent bookstore on the other side of the art gallery touched 3:36, and dark grey clouds loomed. Summer marine layer. Surreal portents. The ghost of Liberty Valance from news to legend. The signal of the sheriff or the outlaws riding to show off. But the imagination stopped because it started to drizzle. There was an awning of course for shade and it served its dual purpose to stop the wet. I turned my head angled hard to face both ends of the road where the blind curves announced and farewelled the commercial patrons. I glanced at a Titian portrait of a Habsburg on the open page, his blank gaze absorbed into mine, and looked blank down the road for a long time.

At 4:15 a man in army fatigues, combat boots, a black shirt, and designer sunglasses strutted into the café. A group of photographers gathered around and as he exited, they sought attention. The action hero in the flesh. The photographers crowded onto the sidewalk and their vocals collided for attention. He took the focus in stride and smiled as if it wasn't staged. He looked at me when he walked by. A familiar face. Maybe a party in the past. Then he came back and shook my hand, "Marcel's friend. From last Saturday." I nodded confirmation. He said, "Have Marcel call me." I couldn't remember his name right away but then it came to me when a trailing photographer cried out, "Dean." Yeah, the All American action hero. A man in motion is the symbol of victory. You stop thinking. You pay attention. You watch the mundane feel significant. After the substitute John Ford showdown, more cars appeared on the road.

The clouds disappeared and the sun was low bent beyond the mountains and the trees. The entire area was cast in a heavy shade so the lighting was more favorable like a celluloid film capture where imperfections hide. The Titian portrait of the Habsburg flipped forward to a map of the Seventy Years War from the hard, cool breeze.

The French girl giggled at the American to my left and the dapper Spanish trio to my right was mixing Irish whiskey with their coffees. I smiled and enjoyed the sentiment. The women with the greyhounds had circled back and it seemed like a long time to spend for a stroll. At the single screen cinema at the far end of the road, a crowd of spectators had lined up. The headline read *I Vitelloni* and the crowd seemed sharper than the standard casual Californian projection. They were quiet, wearing sunglasses, and smoked. All in long pants and long jackets even though the weather was short sleeve acceptable. No children. The French girl with the American decided to get in line and the Spanish trio hailed a livery car. A swarth of boy and girl teenagers replaced them on both sides of me, flooded the area with smoke, but stayed rather composed and behaved rather than speaking over me. Their jovial laughter at the expense of their shared digital thoughts through their cell phones seemed disjointed. Their eyes looked tired yet engaged. They hung around without aim, as I continued to do so, and then peer pretty classmates walked in, and they put away their cell phones. The leader of the rebel pack with the metal band tee shirt and oversized jeans approached the prettiest girl in line and they disarmed in accord. Her friends smiled and gave space. The other girls ordered first and took seats so they could sit with the rebels around me. Popularity and rebellion, a contemporary juxtaposition. Some of the girls looked at me and smiled and I tipped my head.

My car meter showed red, so it was time to go. The shade had morphed into a hard black and the streetlights started to glow. The sky was purple blue from the force of city lights diffusing up from the earth. My body felt baked the way it softens like soft goods left out in the sun for too long, as if I had been a golf kart for three hours and needed a rinse. My cheeks felt sunk and my hair had grease but no residual water curving its free angle. I entered the BMW M5 and time shifted. Like *Two Lane Blacktop* opening shot, open road, justice, American way. The neighborhood seemed filled with ghosts, empty sidewalks, empty pavement. The theatregoers had entered and the café dwellers had shifted indoors. The art gallery stayed alit but the door was closed and the seat outside was removed. I decided dinner was the logical step forward. As a gunshot, I took the road open without a turn signal because the open road is a rare opportunity to satisfy the sequence of entering the vehicle, ignition, and gear shift. Usually, you get in, ignite, shift into drive, and have to wait for the opening, as if you're playing an 8 bar measure, and then you can't fulfill it to completion on the final note. But this time, I could, and I was glad.

I knew Marcel had a refrigerator stocked with Japanese food because he was adamant about its benefits, so I'd partake and understand. I heated up the rice and the mabo tofu mix and arched my back so it cracked. Sitting at that café for so long had a residual effect. I let the food overheat in the microwave and smoked a cigarette so it cooled down in time. I loathed waiting at the microwave. Every time extended to a drag and I deemed myself a base useless animal if I hadn't a task to accomplish at the same time. I hadn't a task, so I smoked. Smoking made me feel in control, like I had a purpose, even if it was death by pleasure. It was chilly outside now, with the darkness and the breeze, so I only smoked half. I stopped the microwave at 3 seconds and had to let the heat smoke to cool. Then I shut the windows but kept the curtains open so I could see the pretty lights grow more prominent as the night fell. I thought of the wine in the cellar but decided on a Nastro Azzurro beer for a few sips before investing in a Kirin Ichiban. Sitting there, alone, enjoying the intake, I seemed to reset and absorb the events. Midweek was coming, Valeria was dead and in the ground, I was exiting the picture, and, at the core, in the cold, alone, my existence was the same as it ever was.

III

I WOKE UP in Tokyo on Thursday. I had caught the red eye Wednesday past midnight, so with the flight, time shift, I'd traveled into the future and lost a day. I wanted to get away and the boss was past caring. He needed me back and when I got back, I'd work hard and he'd be happy, because I always got everything done when it needed to be done. He told me take the week and there's nothing to discuss that couldn't wait. I said I'd make it up to him, and even if I didn't really mean it, it made the phone conversation satisfactory because I recognized and respected his rank. The vocal gesture seemed to fulfill his concerns and it was set, I'd be back Monday.

Japan is the most civil society so far in the course of human development. Granted the administrative labyrinth of the written word and its granularities, the people in and of themselves operate in a superior society, with a social contract reared in respect and collective status quo strength. The technology amplifies that the material result of such a social dynamic maximizes the human element of innovation, efficiency, and quality of life. I passed through customs and greeted the officer with my enthused language skills so he let me go without scanning my eyes. My room wasn't ready for check in so I left my luggage and journeyed around the Imperial Garden. When the sun came out, the humidity went up, so I meandered through the trees. Each step, an American boot, seemed to pierce the ground out of harmony, that I was, in a way, disturbing the serenity of a perfect creation. I smoked in secret, since the new regime had installed smoke booths everywhere in the office buildings and train stations. Some pedestrians walked by but of course they didn't say anything. To maintain a semblance of order, I put out the fire on my boot sole and disposed of the filter in the empty box. I needed more so I went to the convenience store. Then I found a receptacle in the train station and made my way to the Mitsubishi bank headquarters so I could eat gyoza in a restaurant at the base of the building. Japanese food, generally grouped, fills the appetite but doesn't overdo it. You never feel heavy. Just balanced. Clean.

I journeyed to Ginza and stocked up on a variety of foods for my stay. The Mitsukoshi department store depachika food hall on the lower floor is like Harrod's in London. But since I had been to the depachika in Tokyo first, it seemed to me that Harrod's was more like Mitsukoshi. At the back corner, I targeted Johan's bakery. Japanese bakeries give French bakeries a solid competition. I gathered a Deustchesbrot with a wurst wrapped in a soft bread, raisin scattered bread, and then fresh inari sushi, an eel and rice bowl, and the popular tuna cut salad for multiple portions. On the way out, I thought of the chocolates but figured that would wait. The room was ready, technically early, so I checked in and freshened up. I stayed at a business style hotel in the Marunouchi district of Chiyoda City, so it was on top of an office building where American banks had their Tokyo offices. The room included a kitchen and laundry appliances. Naturally, I got a lot done in this environment. A self sustaining unit, overlooking the Imperial Gardens, and without the clouds, Mount Fuji on the horizon.

Showering and taking a nap reset the clock. It was evening but I didn't want to go out, yet I still wanted to feel the pulse of humanity. So, instead of smoking in the dedicated room in the lobby next to the fitness studio, which was usually empty, I went to the ground level of the office building and took the escalator to the subterranean train station where I could smoke in the room amongst the office workers. Diligent, ever working, behaved. Chill. No way to fit in. Even if I was half Japanese, they'd never assume it. *Gai-jin*, foreigner, an outsider. But—American, and American is good, because American is allied. Beneficial mutual interest. Good business. The salarymen cycled in and out of the room with nods and excuse me's, and I had a quick three before reverting up the building to the room. I washed my hands and face, even after I showered. Especially after a shower, washing my face feels like I'm creating a new layer, a new version of myself, a systemic reboot of my machine unit. Maybe it was the environment, the futurescape of Tokyo present through all senses and peripheries, but it felt intense. I'm never intense on the surface, but I felt a genuine sense of peace in such civil surroundings. It was business hours so I checked my mail and forwarded the relevant messages when they needed to be addressed in a timely manner. I had one more cigarette in the smoking room by the fitness studio, and the electrical current through the vending machines bellowed a steady drone and emitted a fluorescent light, like a hospital with tinted accent. I was alone, and at the end, Valeria entered my mind. I had another. She was always in my mind, but when she came to the front, from the backstage, I accepted I was thinking about her and just stood there with it. I felt nothing.

Marcel messaged me at that instant and begged me to come back. He said he had financing for a new picture and that running into Dean at the café was a case of serendipity. That we should work together. I didn't like the idea of compromising the office position for an art project, especially one that I had no idea what it represented. The support of a friend, even in the face of nothing, but with the reminder of death, definitely proves positive. My baseline core was so cold and brutal. Marcel and I had met studying method acting under Lee Strasberg's Institute and, for me, I had not realized the gravity of learning such craft. Serious firepower for being a human, as in, being aware of one's instrument, one's body, one's soul, with the capacity to objectively view myself omniscient. To be conscious of what I'm doing and likewise, disengage from the first person self about the very act of being, not just acting. To displace from the moment because I happen to be programmed to be conscious of what I've compelled my instrument to do and to feel. I'd become a puppet master of myself.

A profound level of self-awareness, to observe my actions and the emotions that serve as their fuselage with an omniscient detachment. I can watch myself navigating situations from the exterior, as if I'm the director of myself as a character on stage, or on set, in a closed controlled environment. It was as if this was activated, like a splitting atom, slowly gathering force in the shadows, upon the method acting training, and it blossomed into a visceral tool, yet, the baseline core seemed so cold and brutal. I'm not in the moment, I'm above it, or outside of it, controlling it. To have mastery of my instrument, to manipulate my emotions and physique, is a skill, I recognize, for it gives the power to approach life with precision and objectivity. The cost, though, seems tragic. The distance from the rawness of human emotion, the vulnerability of being fully in the moment without the haunting conscious detachment. The coldness is strength, it is artillery, it is firepower, but it's a reflection of how deeply I can disengage from feeling in order to maintain control. A superpower, the ability to be both the actor and the director of my own life, deciding when to engage and when to pull back. But am I willing to let myself fully feel, and even if I was willing, has the detachment permanently severed the ability to fully experience certain emotions. The puppet, the puppet master, the duality of irony. More control over life, a greater barrier between me and the act of experiencing outcomes as they occur. The heartless hero, cold. The innocents are massacred by their feelings, naked, instead of being aware of what's internally happening to them. The self mastery of manipulating oneself. Maybe it's a curse. A permanent cold. Emotions drive actions, and if I have no emotions, then what is driving my actions. The absence of emotion is an emotion, yet this cultivated strategic relationship of my mind and body seems more engineered. I am a machinist. I see the full picture, manipulate my internal state, and make conscious decisions about how to engage or detach. Detachment tends to overrule.

That coldness and feeling of being heartless seems the by-product of having learned how to protect myself so well that I consider I may be too far gone, emotionally untouchable. An impenetrable fortress around the emotions that may be too didactically constructed that it is a mystery to breach. A massive edge in terms of resilience and control, yet the sense of isolation and distance from the rawness of life that others seem to experience so openly, plain, and pure. A mastermind of my own psyche, controlling the levers, deciding when and how to feel, and always having the upper hand on the emotional landscape. The disconnect from unfiltered emotional experiences. I didn't choose this. But I chose to study the method. And now, I live with it. It's a dark art I didn't realize the full weight or consequence of, and there's no going back. An animal enchained to the point where there is no need for a cage. Valeria on the stage of my mind. I felt nothing.

I had another cigarette so I didn't have her on my mind any longer. It's better to smoke blank and clear than caught up in some subject beyond control. Then, I slept smooth and had a dream with disjointed relations. When I woke up, I went to the gym. It was still dark out and it felt private because there was no one else. I did the laundry and set up the drying cycle and went for a walk because the dryer was long and weak. The housekeeping staff cleaned my room then and so when I got back, they had also dropped off my mail. I didn't expect any but Marcel had already coordinated a messenger service to deliver a copy of the script the moment I departed for the airport. Three day time seemed impressive for over 5,000 miles. I didn't want to read it so I let it lay on the desk and kept it facedown so I could avoid the title. I stared out the window and saw Fuji peaking through the clouds beyond the glass buildings. Deciding to take a photo, the glass pane made the image seem abstract. But I liked it, the dual layers. In order to take the photo, I had to turn on my phone and use its camera feature. There were voicemails. One more from Marcel persistent that I engage with the material. And another from my colleague at the office. She said a copy of the script arrived at the office and that she put it in my desk, so the boss wouldn't see. I didn't have an agent or a manager but since I was established, I only worked shoots that were in the tax offseason. Given the timing, with the extension deadline approaching, it was better if the boss didn't see it. Even if the boss was my uncle, there wasn't a reason to distract his concentration and consider a scenario farther out into the future. At the end of the message, she said bring me something back. I was going to buy her some snacks anyway but the casual comment was a healthy reminder. Before I showered and napped, I went down to the lobby area for a smoke outside the building. You're not supposed to smoke just anywhere but I did it and saw some white gloved taxi drivers load up with hotel guests to the airport, and a light drizzle came on just as I was finishing the cigarette. A police car screamed by and then the traffic started up again. I caught the elevator door about to close because the Spaniard inside kept it open for me. I had solid energy after the workout and the smokes, and I suppose feeling wanted, getting recruited to be in a new motion picture, involved flattery, validation, and recognition, so I asked the Spaniard how he was doing and how he came to be in Tokyo. He didn't tell me why he was in Tokyo but he said he was well and that he had lived in Los Angeles two years. That's where I had arrived from but not where I came from, not now. I didn't get the time to explain but it didn't matter. He was older and seemed a bit tired, so I walked fast out of the elevator and to the business center so we wouldn't be in the second elevators together to the hotel rooms.

I realized I had forgotten to stock up on rice cracker snacks so I went back down to ground level to cross the street for the convenience store. The crosswalk light started flashing green so I rushed across before I'd be a target for ongoing traffic. The drizzle had stopped and there were construction workers smoking where no one was supposed to. Rare you see Japanese breaking rules. Maybe today was bound to be filled with further surprises. I dropped off the snack stock upstairs and reworked my way to Otemachi Station so I could catch the Marunouchi Line to Tokyo Station. I didn't want to walk because with the drizzle, the humidity was worse. It was unavoidable but it would be worse walking the twelve minutes to Tokyo Station above ground. By the time I arrived at Tokyo Station, I had a sweat but I was laughing because I met my music producer friend who was living in Tokyo on account of his fiancé was a permanent resident. He had pierced his ear and grown out his hair. The pirate aesthetic was suitable. We arrived at Kiji, an Osaka style okonomiyaki restaurant in the commercial center below the JP Morgan building. He was jolly and glad to see an American. We ate like savages. He asked how Los Angeles played out and I told him the context. He said, "It was her journey, and yeah, lucky you weren't in the car." When he put it like that, I stared into the wall and looked back. He was right. He asked if I wanted to go to a day party at the Sky Tower but I didn't feel like meeting and greeting and chatting with new people so I skipped it and walked back to the hotel. My clothes were already layered with the sweat so I figured my legs could use the exercise after the okonomiyaki. On the way back, I saw a lot of salarymen and some loud Chinese tourists by the Imperial Garden. I gazed at the reflecting water by the slate gray walls and over the bridge by the entrance, a couple was taking wedding photos. When I got back, the undergarments, socks, and shirts were dry, so I could shower and finally nap. I had a pack of the rice cracker snacks by Kameda even though I wasn't hungry. It was impulse. Japanese markets in America only sell the knock offs, not the Kamedas, so in Tokyo, naturally, I felt a compulsion to consume the excess.

On my way downstairs for the smoke after the nap, I crossed paths with an English gentleman with a mountain dog. They seemed suitable in stature and dignified airs. We were waiting for the elevator and I asked, "How do you do?" He said, "Just fine, thanks. And you are living here?" I replied naught, that I was a traveler, not a business lodger. The dog appeared virulent and friendly but I noticed a recovering wound on the left foreleg. The gentleman had a similar gash wrapped on his left arm, and I wondered why the coincidence.

They looked a bit like each other the more I noticed, in the best of manners. As if the gentleman's presence had suffused the dog with a relaxed countenance so the leash was mere decorum. Even his hide seemed a bit fabricated in breadth, like a Peter Paul Rubens painting. Just on the exit point at the lobby, he shared his name. Windsor. No wonder. Regal stock. The dog's name, I don't remember, but they were a singular unit, minds unified. Very compatible within the homogenous Japanese land. He said he'd see me again at this time or on the morrow early if fate so played its hand to our pleasure. A business lodger not dictated by the office hours of Chiyoda City. No wonder yet again. Executive branch. I let him go to the ground floor and went to the isolated smoking room by the fitness studio.

It wasn't isolated because I showed up. There was a Belgian couple, but the woman was half French half Dutch. The man was much older than her. She was my age and she was taller than me. He was our father's age. We all smiled. Nodded our heads. He excused himself and then me and her just stood there until she asked me for a light since he had taken it. I asked her « Ça va, mademoiselle? »[1] laying on an immediate casual pretense. She said « Ça va. »[2] I went on, « J'espère que je ne vous dérange pas, si on parle un peu pendant les cigarettes. »[3] Elle a dit, « Bien sur » et on continuait comme une air détendue et très, très cool. J'ai vu sa bague et puis notre yeux nous a traversé le monde et partagé une tension.[4] I switched to English. "He'd kill me, wouldn't he?" She did the same. "No, it'd be a crime of passion and it'd be me, but typically, he wouldn't say a thing if I didn't say a thing. That way, it would be meaningless." I raised an

---

1   "How's it go, Miss?"

2   "So it goes."

3   "I hope I'm not a bother to you, if we talk a bit during the cigarettes."

4   She said, "Of course," and we continued like a relaxed air and cool, very cool. I saw her and then our eyes crossed the world and shared a tension.

eyebrow and took a deep drag. She lived off him, clearly not working, even if she was entrepreneurial. I gathered modern women in the age of education and opportunity have proven potent and formidable in capital enterprise, contingent upon requisite financing options. She mentioned it. « J'ai mon propre entreprise de la mode, mon nouveau collection est en toutes les magasins du Japon. Alors, on y va ici pour moi. »[5] I said, what about a stroll, would he wonder, and she said, no, he's sleeping, I'll message him though, so when he wakes up, he knows.

If he's double her age, it's not a big deal. Of course, it may be a foolish business decision. Nevertheless, I hadn't decided. I was a gun. Direct in front. If I was shot, I'd hit the target. And a European beauty in a Japanese setting is surrealism with allure. I knew who I was and what I liked and accepted the actions as a byproduct of my desires. The consequences were best suppressed by a laissez faire mentality. Doing what I was doing without judgment. Was I a scoundrel? No. Just an animated beast with a capacity to structure thoughts into semantic constructs, utilize tools and systems, and fancy myself in control of my own destiny on the axiom that reason and logic sculpt control and power. We played along for pleasure but I wouldn't actually do a thing. I'm always the good guy, by role, even if what goes on in my mind is base, carnivorous, and lewd. She didn't know where the limit was and that was part of the rush. Crossing cultures is a proving ground for mystery versus real action. Eye to eye, who blinks. My hands don't shake but my interior stirred. I wanted her, especially here, but I didn't want to play the role for follow through. I stayed on talk and she invited me to a trunk show for the new collection at a nice store in Aoyama. Actually planning on going to the Nezu Museum that day to sit in the garden and sedate my mind, maybe I would stop by, but I shouldn't. Of course I didn't say this out loud.

---

5   "I have my own fashion company, my new collection is in all the shops of Japan. So, we go here, for me."

Then everything changed. She said, "You see, Monsieur Reuter, it's not that I'm a kept woman, but I have needs. A man says to me, 'If you're ready, let's go, perhaps I'd take him up on his offer.' I'd say, 'Take me there, but take it easy.' Then the man would say, 'I'm cool, but you have my heart racing.' Then I'd laugh and warn him that once he decided to go down this road, there's no backing out." We were in front of Tokyo Station at the huge plaza and the sky was changing from evening to night. He'd probably be up already, and hesitation boiled my insides. She gave me an out. It hadn't been an immediate imperative, but she wanted the window open tomorrow after the Aoyama show and my Nezu sojourn. I wanted to tell her a story in an eloquent manner but I just replayed it in my head through experience before I said another word. We smoked and had a break from the breaths held and the words spoken, and this was nice, standing next to each other, in the shade, as the sky started to sleep under the moonlight.

The story I'd tell was about a girl in New York who didn't have a sister, but I wish she had one. And how we were friends, platonic, yet I thought otherwise, and we acted the romance without the consequences, so there was no literal regret. And there were no regrets. But I never saw her again, and I didn't want to see her again. A symbol of my own wild horse nature before the fall of youth into the agenda suicide of office work balance life. She didn't resemble this Famke but the scenario was a natural trigger. I thought of what I considered such thoughts would merit. Blood, violence, a duel for many acts less threatening and more honorable. For I had never breached that land of the underground upon which there is no going back, and the mirror never lies. So I imagine, so I continue to imagine, and so I shall retain composure to never lose myself and find myself across that border. The allure of dark and mysterious, even though my skin was pretty pale, the hair and eyes had a brood about them that projected bestiality to the fairer sex. I held the firm conviction that physical attraction had an underlying basis in internal purity and karma, for energy morphs the body into composition, like a plant immersed in sun and water. The phenomenon of creation. She had an intuition that I was thinking of another woman.

She demanded to know. I didn't want to kill her fantasy and spoil the charm, so I had to sidestep around by offering her one of mine in exchange for a Galouise. She didn't fall for the easy fix, to just ask about her shoes, and scent, and general visual upkeep. She knew what I was doing. She looked great knowing what I was doing. The natural ease of presence in the most civilized society had me in a good mood as a baseline. I was nicer because the environment was nicer. I was more enthused because the social fabric was more enthused. George Washington wrote a letter about civility. Americans forget. I'm American no matter what. American programming, the origin of my mind. So even I forget when I go back. There are some aftershocks and permanent perspective shifts but the overall attitude conforms to the system in which one must operate. Avoiding the system is not healthy. Integration is necessary for growth. But so she kept on in a makeshift maneuver. She inquired as to why I did not have a girlfriend. I told her I was in Los Angeles for a funeral and that I was here as a respite before a return to the office and such pace. The connection was not apparent, but I framed it in this fashion so it'd strike with brute force. I said, "Well, the funeral was for a girl from childhood who was in love with me." She broke eye contact and then looked back with a subtle smile. Deep smoke drag. Tension displacement. The conversation had progressed to where there was more detail than necessary, especially for a casual encounter. Yet, I know the mysterious brood presents opportunity for discovery and I'm a natural exhibitionist. I enjoy the intellectual probing just as much as the mind hunter. It's an art, to reveal a sliver of the picture and a path through the labyrinth. The reluctant hero. Anti. By luck or just pure symbiotic chemistry, she chose to share facets of her story with me so we could lower the intensity and maintain the seductive equilibrium. She was thrice divorced, and here I revealed I was an accountant for estates and trusts, American concentrated.

She invited me to have a coffee and cigarettes so she could ask some advice. I sat on a couch and she brought a chair straight on to me and crossed her legs. Inspection. I braced for a femme fatale strategy and got comfortable. All her husbands had American passports except the current and she had inherited estate tax exemptions from them all but the third had a larger unused exemption amount than the previous two, so she was in good standing. It was unlawful to have a perpetual cumulative estate tax exemption, as in she could hypothetically keep adding to her unused tax exemption for each subsequent death. It was always limited to one. But she plainly stated she had 3 qualified interest terminable property trusts from all three deceased spouses and that the children had enough funds in trust that they sought naught to attack her through litigation. I smiled and commented she had quite a strategic implementation for security. But now she was no longer living in the United States and she wished to no longer be deemed tax resident. I erred on the side of caution for the expatriation tax because the security of an established relationship with the United States is one not to be lightly considered. The ultimate military power in the West, the primary failsafe for liberty and land volume. A self sustaining superpower. The simple and harsh reality was to liquidate the American retirement funds, pay capital gains tax on the sales of the bonds and equities, and transfer the cash to a non American trust. If she was prudent with her investment discipline, she could split the assets between a British commonwealth island tax haven, the Cayman Islands, the Isle of Man, and then concentrate a portfolio in Switzerland, which has high fees but literal physical fortress security and institutional hospitality. Nevertheless, it was wise to maintain the greatest concentration of assets in the United States, the original QTIP trust from the original spouse, because his portfolio of American securities was already serviced by JPMorgan, Goldman Sachs, and the Bank of New York held custody. She had American, Dutch, and Belgian passports. She was a Dutch national but had married American and Belgian, so she maintained her birth citizenship. She remained cautious about the States, but she knew that deep down, paying the expatriation tax and having no way back heightened her risk portfolio in an ever evolving world. I reassured her I could set her up with attorneys in Bern, who I had hired as consultants, given the nature of my cross border tax work based in Zürich. Of course, I was American, and an American security apparatus is the most ubiquitous, regardless of how one prefers to have their services presented through language, customs, and faces. I reiterated to take my words at face value, for I had nothing to gain, other than the pleasure of her company, along with an informed opinion that may or may not be the most knowledgeable given I was an accountant and did not provide legal counsel. I had an ethical imperative to uphold the tax codes and provide the utmost tax advice that could benefit my clients through legal tax avoidance procedures. American general and president Eisenhower had said plans are useless, but planning is essential. It was all in the nature of planning. We shifted our conversation to the capital markets, and macroeconomics, the central banks, and a general malaise with the global financial system. Stronghold balance sheet states with liquid currencies were the best. Hence, the United States, the dollar, Switzerland, the franc, Japan, the yen, and the United Kingdom, the pound sterling. The Euro was liquid but there was a lot of variability in the geopolitical landscape, given the diversity of the players. It would be wise to have side by side deposits in Canada and Australia, because their currencies were a hedge against the vagaries of global capital markets, per their economic engines driven by commodities and petroleum. Geographic diversity and characteristic quality was equally important to technology and infrastructure. Germany had it all, but it was like a Promethean Atlas holding up the Eurozone post the 20th Century Thirty Years War, and with American military a permanent presence, it paid a phantom tax for diplomatic trust and cooperation. The Deutsch mark was solid, but that was in the past. The Italian lira was actually solid, but there was too much tax evasion in that country. And France, while Paris was a crown jewel, was America with a more rebellious labor force. Plus, she had Euros in The Netherlands and Belgium. She brushed off Monaco because it was too small. She said she already had funds in lower lands, and didn't like the idea of more coastal caches, given the rising tides, and general instability of an ocean vulnerable locale. I raised my eyebrows and said it was actually solid, lax, and low key, but she hadn't the desire. I didn't get far enough to mention Singapore, United Arab Emirates, Hong Kong, or the ultimate opportunities, South America and Africa, because she disarmed and went on a monologue. She said paying for advice deems it difficult to discern between substance and a charlatan selling a bill of goods. She asked for my business card, and I shared, so now, she knew my name and identity. I hadn't known hers. Exposure. I said in another life, maybe New York. Her textile mills were in Italy already, she had factories in Hungary, and her enterprise was already in Switzerland, so she just wondered the best mechanism for her to solidify her personal assets, independent and clear from the business. She should have had already significant counsel, but as she stated again, she wanted an objective viewpoint from someone with no moneys to gain. Just a luck of the draw, finding a real accountant in Japan of all non English speaking jurisdictions. I said my last piece, that most people stay dependent on the system they've been programmed to operate within, but the global approach, high and low, enables destiny control. And the best position, in the here and now, and through the rest of our lifetimes, with all military reality accepted, is American with cross ocean options.

She was ready to have a go at it, and I really didn't want to go there. Her husband was definitely awake by now, but she wanted confirmation for tomorrow. I agreed so she'd get off my back, but I didn't plan on following through. I had the Nezu and she had the Aoyama trunk show, but I'd devise a way out. It may have been Arete's last gasp before Hedone sent Bacchus for victory's wine. I could tell she wanted another beer so I took her up on it, even if we had been spending more time together than we had expected. She said she hadn't told me everything, and I clearly knew, but it was preferable to pause before the reveal the next time I'd see her. I drank the decaf because it tasted brisk and made me focus as placebo. Another trade, a Galouise for an American Spirit, and a touch of the hand when she handed me back my flame. She went and got a muffin and we shared it in silence. She sat next to me on the couch and our forks clashed. She said she knew what people thought of her. That she was a tramp, that she was a gold digger, an opportunist. Of course she was an opportunist and she was materially driven, but not because she didn't have to start. It was just she accepted it with full bravado and rather than conform to a repressed sense of self, she sought bigger and bolder. Her enterprise was growing and she was doing it without her own inheritance. I caught her Icarus wings a nudge before she went on fire, and noted her education, place of birth, and familial protection, gave her a springboard that was irreplicable. She shouldn't deny the truth. She looked at me hard. I was right. Deep down, I couldn't help but speculate on coming to relational terms with a woman of her knowledge and prowess. It'd be a perpetual mind game with potential calamity and swindle. Maybe that was my imagination on account that I'd seen too many film noir pictures and read too many of their fountainhead psychological novels. A modicum lackluster for an innocence lost in paradise. But that was a trite fantasy, for she was married, and she had singular ambitions. I'd only be a passenger in her vehicle, and her driving, while notably commendable worldwide, was more a menacing danger than a welcoming warrior. Unless I really was one of Lucifer's followers after the fall. I kept telling myself otherwise. It's only requisite to consider the alternative, circa Milton. An absolute is a fascist regime. A rebel is a pure heart. But if you mix terms and cast blame on the same rebel, then it creates confusion because there are contradictory systems governing the terms. Good versus evil, or fascism versus freedom. If Lucifer is evil and free, yet

God is good and fascist, then the recipe for evil pervades and gestates because the sycophants that have institutionalized these flawed precepts are unequivocally more concerned with sating their base greed and taste for power. The human element.

She was a cheater, and sure, I was the same age and so we had some equal leveling, but I couldn't deny her capability. She said, "It's an arrangement. In the time where I unify with a peer, similar age range, aligned interests, general needs, I'd come into my own, as a woman." Her ex-husbands and current husband paid the lodging fees and taxes and provided her with an allowance for activities. She maintained all equity in her pursuits and so, was building off balance sheet. She emphasized she was not a gluttonous nymph, that her pursuits were creative, productive, giving something back. Of course she had a penchant for fine dining, luxury goods, and pleasant holidays, but these were release points from a steady ambitious drive of work, endeavor, and purpose. Her neighbors were typical, in that they refused to work. They complained they had not enough jewels, pocket books, shoes, gowns. A deepening melancholy ascending the battle of life for the opposing team had chosen not to play. The choice of no station is a deep risk. Granted, she noted she had a few mentor neighbors, elder stateswomen that managed their households with tact and efficiency, a sharp edge governing their husbands, who were all of comparable age. She was the young gun, and she learned fast. The ones who complained of funds. They were the cheaters. She was the businesswoman. She was young, and she had needs. When she had kids, it would become real.

It had to be someone like me. She had identified me as a potential suitor. This, I was assured. I didn't need her. She didn't need me. The best of dynamics. I wouldn't have to provide the money. It'd be a mutual accord. I didn't blame her. I realized I admired her ability to execute. She was dangerous. Smarter than me. I felt not threatened. Intrigue. She'd witnessed many transfers of assets, and those above her in rank, wealth, experience, age, had prepared for the inevitable in these scenarios. Her insider exposure to such wealth management was akin to my tax experience. I rationalized she was not just note, but perhaps, worthy in totality. A femme fatale seeking a life with a white knight, a pure heart. She told me he was cheating on her, too. She preferred labeling the dynamic as playing around, having his fun, passing time with other women. Cheating had such a dramatic flare. The word. The confrontational characteristic. She had found tickets to the Philharmonic in his smoking jacket interior pocket. They were seats too good for a friend. Recent following, she'd found a receipt from the Maison Goyard shop on Rue Saint-Honoré. He was on a leisure trip while she was in business meetings in Paris. They were a going concern. He didn't mind what she chose to do, as long as she maintained the status quo. She wasn't malicious, nor was he. He liked her company and her commanding presence. I could understand. Of course, I lacked the paternal framework, for we were the same age. We had no children. I told her she was interested in me. She laughed as in Versailles court, a voilà. She told me: "You don't realize how good you already have it with me. Tomorrow you'll know just how good it can be. And next time."

Her words were blade sharp. It seemed like she hadn't said this before. Like I was special. She continued, "I'll suck you dry, until your eyes bleed, and you'll scream inside. Your blue blood will flow red to me. It all ends the same. If you ask what I want, don't worry. I want you. Don't overthink."

This turn of situational awareness seemed heightened. The flare for drama in my life seemed at a peak. I was tired, but this was stimulating to my ego and the steady rhythm. How could I deny playing into her arms? I enjoyed feeling wanted and knowing I was wanted from such a confident person. I felt human. Maybe I did care, at the core, though I would play it off as another reinforcing experience that my ego was justified. She wanted more advice but I wasn't up for it. She set back her desire. She implied she could dissect my mind's eye when we would be in bed. She had sexual feelings for me.

She did not want to quell those for the professional upkeep. After the trunk show, she said we'd take a taxi back to the hotel and there'd be no scandal. There is no underworld threat of scandal in Japan. The Yakuza regulate the street and we were foreigners. Sure I had a Hollywood connection but there wasn't a bother at such vast distance from the epicenter. What she wanted and how she achieved her objectives was through discretion. I was still thinking about it. I figured the longer I played with the idea, the more probable I'd go along with her direction. Straight ahead, the gun couldn't miss. She still wanted to ask me something. Before she did, though, she couldn't help but try to pry it out of me without a direct inquiry. What I had thought of the matter in Los Angeles. Of the girl that was in love with me. Of her death. Of my state of mind. Of my heart. I read her mind. There was so much distance but so much connection in our eyes. I knew what she wanted. And I wanted to give it to her. She just had to say she wanted to ask me something. And I'd give her the answer without her asking. The art of tennis. Back and forth. I said I didn't feel anything more than what I had already felt. That it was a lost cause. That I had left her before and I had no regrets. It worked out the way I directed it to work out. But the death, of course, was a sad affair. A high impact evisceration of future happenstance. I didn't foresee it ever coming to pass that we would rework together. Even if it was gone, I still wished her the best and for her to be happy on her journey, even if it was without me. But straight up, in the moment, now, I felt nothing. I thought she was foolish for having made the decisions she'd made to construct her life into the resultant outcome that she had achieved. A sordid marriage, a plain mediocrity. A melancholy oblivion. It wasn't about her, so much as it was, and always was, and is, about me. I knew I was the better person for her. I was the better person for anyone. I could fulfill the grand dream made real. I had loved her for 23 years, since the first day of sixth grade. Sure life had taken turns and I hadn't seen spoken to her in seven years, seen her in ten. Regardless, even if there was a fading of surface presence, it was never resolved. I had thrown a bold declaration of love before her marriage those seven years ago, that I would love her forever. I was young and bold and naïve to the bolt of human emotion. But she had made her decision and chosen her fate. I was alone and I kept on. It was my fault. I had left her those years ago because she had no dreams. She was dead inside. I couldn't see past the belief that she could come alive. But that was my flaw. Thinking she had to change. She was who she was. And I loved her still for who she was, even if it wasn't what I thought she could become. Becoming and being are slivers of the same composite. But talking to the live audience right now, all I could say was I felt nothing. For that was the truth. The situation spoke for itself. It was over.

She took a deep gulp of her beer. Then she finished the muffin. She took it. She didn't ask if I wanted a last bite. I liked that. She wanted what she wanted and wasn't afraid. Then from her purse, she took out a piece of paper and wrote her number down with a red pen. When she wrote her full name down, I knew she was old money. The cursive, the 'Van der' spaced out, not combined into a singular name. Some duchess or countess in direct descendance. She gave me a piece of blank paper and the red pen, so I'd provide an exchange. I accepted what was to come to pass because I was having such a good time letting her direct the scenario. I suppose she had won me over. And even if I felt nothing about what had passed in Hollywood, I admitted it was a blessing to have a connection with a Western woman in such a civilized exotic locale. I had dreamed of being here with a worthy connection, in romance, in love, and even if we weren't quite there yet, the substitute was clearly candidate level in substance and atmosphere. I read my name out loud and the phone number because it had repeating digits and sounded pleasant in English. She stood up and I followed her outside as she lit a cigarette. She asked me to read the number again. I did. She recited it in memory at an instant. An easy to remember number, sure, but still flattering that she'd taken the effort to successfully instill it into memory. She was good with numbers. Management. Wealth. She traded her number for mine and kissed the sheet I gave her. A suave move. "Nice penmanship," she remarked. I said, "Likewise." "Now you're mine, Reuter." She had stopped calling me "Mister." I was disarmed. She was at ease. A pause in the concrete desert. No cars went by. A silent suspense. Her looking down the way, the smoke a sign of the time passing. I smoked mine, too, and we didn't say anything for a while, enjoying the silence. Then the waves of cars resumed and the sounds of tires against concrete hummed like sand on a morning tide. She asked my age, and I immediately answered, "Thirty-four." She responded that time moves faster than we realize. This was true. The love of my childhood was dead. I was in Tokyo with a childless beauty. She was married, but that would end. Would I seize this moment for what it could become? She finished, "It's good that you feel nothing. Otherwise, I'd think you were held up. But now that you're not, you'll probably fall in love with me. And I'd like that."

I finished my cigarette and looked down as I put it out. I looked back up and she was smiling at me cool and then she shut her lips and stared strident. An assured gaze. A perfect face. She looked quick. "I feel like you're my friend." I had instant accord. "Just friends." She said, "Quite." She held a cigarette in her lips and kicked her chin back in jest. She didn't light it. There was all intrigue. She sealed the note with the phone number and put it in her jean pocket. A folded treasure. Future opportunity. I must have looked tired because well, I was, I wanted to take a nap. She said let's head back and I said I'm already going that way. She said nap time, and we were aligned in thought and mood. She said don't let it get to me. I said it wasn't, but there was a defensive posture. "It's only natural. You are human. But it'll pass. Especially, you are talking to me." I smiled diffident, but, overall, and through the moment, she had a point. She explained that my narrative of Hollywood and social ties was beyond my control and that all I could control was my actions going forward. That good things were bound to happen to me. She emphasized again, "You are talking to me." I said, "I'm glad we are." In the most unexpected of places. She asked why I was here in the first place. I paused and we stood at the crosswalk by the bank headquarters and the Imperial Gardens. This was good so I could look her direct in the eyes. "I'm half Japanese, even if I don't look it. When I come to Japan, I get a reset, like the world is in order. Like I'm in order. All is clear." Before she could say it, I said it, "Especially now that I'm talking to you." She pecked me on the cheek. It was genuine. She made it so and we both knew.

We went up the elevator. She gave me a hard handshake and said until tomorrow. She said point blank, "We understand each other." I asked what time was the trunk show, she told me, and I said I'd be in the area. She stood outside the elevator because she was on the 27th floor and I was still going up to the 29th. She blew me a kiss and let the doors close. She said she'd send me a text message and that she'd meet me at the Nezu Museum garden. When I got to the 29th floor, the cold hallway was clean and well lit, like all modern hotels. I could hear housekeeping down the hallway arranging laundry and speaking in muffled tones. My heart was pounding from the moments past but I maintained an air of calm on the surface. I approached my hotel room with the keycard in hand, and stood there for a second before entering, as I was crossing a threshold and life would change. I thought of the Freya at the beach, and Famke here now, and of the lost love dead, and it seemed good things were happening to me. I brushed off considering if I deserved them. Down the hallway, the sound of a door opening and guests breaching the silence. I went in and put the concern to rest. The sun shown all the way from Mount Fiji through the buildings to penetrate the bedroom. I sighed softly and accepted the manifestation.

IV

I SLEPT IN PEACE without dreams. I woke and worked out hard in the fitness studio. Marcel called me and was adamant about reading the script. I looked at how long it was, 95 pages, and decided, I'd look at it on the plane. I still had a day left in Tokyo and rather enjoy the moment. He asked what I could possibly be doing and I said I met a girl. He was happy that I was not hung up and that I should live my life. Holding onto the past gets you nowhere. This was profound and her journey was over. Mine had a new lifeline. Famke sent me a photo of herself before the trunk show and I made sure I was well fed and energized for the day ahead. I stopped by a Japanese fashion store through Omotesando after wading through the labyrinth of Harajuku's quiet border streets. The good looking Japanese looked like Elves from Middle Earth, alien but beautiful. No perspiration, no flaws, just defining features and a grounded presence, immortal. In the Nezu garden, I made my way downhill to the pond and zoned out for ten minutes. The past, present, future all collided into one instance and my phone vibrated with an alert from a message from Famke. I kept using her name in my internal dialogue. She was a person now and I looked forward to seeing her. I admit I was even excited. As a schoolboy after lunch ready for the mystery of romance.

  She snuck up on me. It was endearing. A real smile. Seeing the other couples, tourists, families, made the moment feel more grounded and genuine. There was a cool breeze and her hair brushed over her left eye, a nymph in a Bouguereau painting. Our moment together seemed more like a Fragonard painting scene, an allure of love and courtship coming into being. We held hands for a moment and kissed serene. She read my palm and said my future was fortunate. She said she'd teach me how and I wondered when. A child skipped a rock on the pond, breaching the peace, but it seemed fitting. As the waves refracted and scattered a cool momentum, I put my arm around her hips and drew her closer to me so we were one entity. I chewed some gum to get a rush of cool because the cigarettes from before meeting made my throat dry. I couldn't smell a thing but the intention was clear. She put her lips forward and we caught the sunlight when I put mine on hers. Her tongue released a layer on mine and we swayed in each other's arms with the passing breeze as the waves went to sleep.

We took a Mercedes taxi car to Chiyoda City and when she walked ahead of me and looked back, her eyes beamed with light and innocence. A city constructed garden of Eden with an angel leading me through paradise. We went to my room. I had tidied up. We didn't say anything. It was all happening. I suppose I had wanted to her to see me with representative objects. Nothing reveals your personality more than the way you keep your living quarters. Sure I left the script there, folded over. It wasn't a priority. The History of the Habsburg Empire book stacked on top, so the binding and title were visible. I was on the verge of writing a new novel and the emotions of the recent events had mixed into a compulsive brood. I knew it was coming and I had armed myself with time and clean space. I had had full stock of fresh seafoods and baked goods from Mitsukoshi Ginza's food hall and had claimed the hotel space as my own. My utility of the space, adaptable anywhere. After we showered and got into bed and went through the dance, we laid there together. We didn't speak any words from that point. I held her in my arms and enjoyed her hair brushing against my chest. Her bosom felt warm and I was welcome in embrace. I thought room service but decided we'd share some bread from Johan's bakery and a fresh cut tuna salad. I knew I liked her. If I had an appetite after the physical, it meant I was actually attracted. Reinforcing the energy of life together. I didn't want a cigarette, death. I wanted life, the pleasure of health. Her mother called her and she didn't want to blow her off, so I went and had a cigarette in the lobby smoking room by happenstance. In the elevator on the way back up, I saw my Indian neighbor who was in extended residence at the hotel for a foreign assignment. After walking down the hallway together and parting ways at the perpendicular, I made my way inside. No speech but a classical Mozart piano was coating the room in serenity. I asked Famke about the trunk show in detail and was interested in her analysis of the ordeal. She propositioned a walk around the block and I took her up on the offer. The sun was cascading through the clouds like half open blinds and she walked ahead of me strident, the spotlight jumping on and off her face through each sunspot. I got to the details of the script and how I had avoided getting into it until the plane back to *Zürich* and she was intrigued by the Hollywood ties. Marcel was a big name she had heard of and her eyebrows raised when she recognized him for who he was to me, and who I was, in the context of the Hollywood machine, in general. I didn't want to get into too much deep forest about it because Hollywood has a tendency to mask the big picture for the labyrinth of confusion that it embodies by its very nature. The mystique and allure are persuasive tactics for attraction but the reality of it is more nuanced and quite brutal. I suppose it's a matter of perspective and given my background raised in its corridors, I was a bit numb to its effect. We had made the full lap back to the hotel and outside the grand glass entrance doors, she lit a cigarette. I complied. She went down the small side street where the plants framed the stone path and the pathway lights were coming on for the evening. She posed like the Vogue cover girl she truly was and I wanted her there, alone and forever. She cast profile and looked my way. She asked if I loved her. I broke eye contact and looked at her neck before reestablishing gaze. I told her it didn't matter and that I didn't know. Even if I did, I said, I wouldn't tell her. It was too soon. She said a casual love is still a love. I said I didn't think so. She laid on that the word itself has a power but there's more power in saying it, even for a moment that may pass and fade. I didn't say it. She looked down. When she looked up, her eyes were sad. Then she smiled at me and the cigarettes were done, so I approached her. We kissed and it was real. Then police cars flew by with their sirens and a gust of wind rushed into the corridor. A taxi van backed in adjacent to us and that was our signal to go in.

At the elevator a couple was arguing in a Slavic language. They were very elegant in dress but they seemed to be losing class by the moment. Then they cut into English, as if they wanted us to understand the context. "How could you?" said the woman in gown and jewels. The man in scarf and sport coat said, "I don't know what you mean." She said it didn't matter and she walked off. He went after her. Famke and I looked at each other and then at their narrowing shadows. The elevator doors opened. After her I followed and we went up. We didn't acknowledge what we had witnessed but then I said it. "When are you going to leave him?" The doors opened and she said, "It depends on you." She got out and looked back. She said, "Call me, let's go to Milan. Fashion week, I have a show." I said I'd be there even if I wasn't sure. It felt too good to be true. I let her go ahead and take the elevator from the lobby to her floor. Instead of going up, I had one more smoke in the lobby chamber. I realized I just had these smokes to pass the time, to instill some purpose. It was terrible for me, sure, I could feel and see that, but I hadn't let it go. I consciously considered I'd quit for good once I got truly unified with a woman, that that was it. Love, marriage, kids, the whole story. I almost decided I should read the script when I got back to the room but I went for a shower and nap instead. When I awoke, I went to the fitness studio before dinner. Mount Fuji was disappearing into the darkness on sunset and the lights of the foreground buildings made me think of an animated cartoon, as if the impression of reality was so impactful that reality itself came to be defined by its very inspiration. I didn't want to smoke but I put the script in my carry on so it wouldn't tempt me. Then a knock at the door.

It was her. Who else was I to expect? She looked rather distraught. Of course this was the first I'd seen of this mood. She came in like she owned the place. But she still smiled innocent like she was from a small village. I didn't clarify but I assumed and felt natural to be the protective presence. She didn't hug me. She walked by into the hallway and washed her face in the bathroom. Then she came out, sniffled some into a tissue, and sat at the desk. I kept standing and waited for the story. "Yeah, a fight." I moved it along, "Happens sometimes." "Especially when traveling," she kept on. He didn't hit her but he might have. That's what she kept reiterating. I said he didn't seem like the type, and he wasn't, according to her, but it didn't matter, now that she felt that way. It wasn't the body language, she claimed, but the malice in his eyes. It wasn't because of us, I questioned, and it wasn't. It was beyond us. It was something else. He was still in love with his ex-wife and he couldn't take it no longer. She didn't want to process it, even though she never loved him. She told him that, and he stopped caring. The intensity had faded but it was done. She was leaving him. I didn't want to take this on now. Timing was pierced. If I had to deal with her on the level of serious commitment at this point in time, I wasn't ready. I said I wasn't the answer. She said she knew, but she needed a sounding board. I accepted that. Only human. I thought of making a joke about another beneficial trust coming her way accelerated but I passed on the moment. Her eyes looked focused like a warrior and it was wiser to let her dictate where we were going. I went to the kitchen and got her a glass of water. She looked at me, appreciative, and took a long drink. Then a deep breath. She had settled. Calm, cool, collected, just like that. I respected her grit. We didn't say anything for more than a moment. I said I was going to shower. She nodded and laid on the bed and stared at the glowing skyline.

Showering is a private meditation. You enter the portal, clear out the mind and body, and a new scene is established. A new version. She was where she was before and now sleeping. She looked at peace. It was comfortable. Natural. I repressed the affectation. My affection was firm but the timing, again, the timing, was too soon. I hadn't the desire to dive right in. I looked in the mirror by the desk.

Was I a fool? What trick was beyond my foresight? Or was it my own limitations as a man? I had proven so hardened that my baseline analysis was a killswitch. The heart was the heart but she couldn't be it. Even if she was a dream. She had ambitions, objectives, and she was living them out, on her terms. She didn't need me, and I loved that. Not about her, but about any woman. There was no pretense. I was de facto attracted on a physical plane. I could eat with her. No make-up. And moreover, her personality was brawn, brash, and elegant. I almost admitted I felt assured, but I could play into any scenario. My enthusiasm was subdued. She was a married woman. Over time, with maturation, and age dynamics, it didn't matter. But at the core of the social contract, of course it mattered. Now that it was disintegrating, she was open to the future. My future was wide open, but I liked keeping it that way. The German girl in Los Angeles went across my mind. That was just as natural. It was less tension, less suspense, but clearly a real connection. She sent me a message that she'd be in Milan the same time, for the catwalk. Convergence creates anticipation. I could take the train from Zürich. All would be clear but I was sorry about that. It'd be clear for each of them, in each of their spheres of reference, but for me, it'd create conflict. I'd have to choose. Was I ready to make a choice? My standard action was none. I had my fun and embraced the moments blessed by the powers beyond sight and reason and took them in stride. Playing it cool has its limits. Famke was still asleep there, but there was no question. I wanted Freya. Famke woke up. She wanted to stay but she knew she should go. I kept reading on about Wilhelm I and his ascension. The picture had changed. She wasn't hungry but I ate almost everything I had left. I said I was going back to Ginza to get more. She left at six o'clock. Instead of going, I decided I wouldn't smoke. I slept for a few hours.

Around nine o'clock I got a call from my friend Nicky. He was the musician who was engaged to a Japanese girl and lived in Tokyo. He was still in town. He said he was downstairs and invited himself up. A knock on my door and he came in. He poured himself a glass of water and took a Kameda rice cracker snack packet and sat at the desk. He didn't say anything so I asked him how it all was. He told me that he was on the rocks with his girl but he knew his life was better with her and he wouldn't do anything to risk what he had with her. He emphasized this had been the longest time they had spent together and that they needed larger accommodations. I could see the rest of the scenario. I told him it seemed to me he was a big boy and given he had set up a studio at home, another room was essential. Then, it'd all smooth over. It was natural. Respect of space and time. I emphasized he ought to be happy. She was in his life and he was better for it. He agreed and he repeated that he ought to be happy. He was he said then, but that I should know, there are waves to the emotions. He said her sister came by a lot and just having guests made the space smaller and restrictive. He pointed out he'd step up and it would be settled. I asked when the wedding was and he was vague. I said I didn't like the idea of marriage unless it made sense. He knew he could talk to me because I was a solo operator that had stayed the course until my affairs were in order. Even if my affairs were unconventional, my motivations still aligned. The romance, the adage of unity, the dream made real. I said I didn't expect anything and that when the opportunity met preparation, I'd act on it. Just like what he was doing. I underscored. He shook my hand and finished his glass of water. I told him about Hollywood and he said she was on her journey. It's a shame it had to go the way it did but that's the nature of the beast. She was on her journey. It was so simple yet it felt so profound, his ease and assurance in statement. He seemed upbeat and proposed a walk and feast. I put myself together, washed my face, got the right shoes and a light jacket for the breeze. He said he'd buy ahead of time and I wasn't sure what to say, so I just went along with his consideration. We went to this underground gyoza spot under the Mitsubishi bank building a few blocks away. We both agreed our prospects were bright.

The camaraderie of men made me feel honorable. There was

no pretense, other than letting the crawl of ego occasion itself to differing opinions. There was none of that now. He bought me a Kirin Ichiban beer. Then he wanted to go to a night time party in Kabukicho where his associate was spinning vinyl records. I felt like we were in the same loop as at the okonomiyaki place and him seeking my company for the Tokyo Sky Tower day party. I didn't want to change the course of events, so I kept my stance, and said I rather get some sleep. Stay on my course of sleep, early wake, fitness, and dance with the machine. He chided. There would be girls. I didn't tell him about Famke with specifics but I said I already had had a date. He didn't inquire more. He just knew I was who I was. We took our time walking back to the hotel and he waited while I had a smoke outside. He told me how glad he was that he could talk to me about his living dynamics and that he felt positive about the future sharing his concerns and realizing they were solvable with relative ease. I said what I had said to myself out loud. Control my actions and thoughts. Be myself. Be a good person. Good things happen to me. I found his smile very welcoming. He accepted my self professed mantra, struck hands, saluted farewell, and I thought it was an authentic experience etched into memory.

Famke didn't message me. She was strong and I was sure she was working out what she had to face. You eat what you kill. She had to know this was a transition. She was at the edge of her world and in the face of a new glacier. A viking with no one in sight. I was a semblance of an anchor, a foggy hope in some future where she could rediscover some stability. I didn't want to commit. There was a rain shower outside with thunder and a lightning strike by a concentration of buildings. I considered my regiment. Lift, body weight. Farmer's walks for grip strength. Long slow intervals, the elliptical, runs, resistance. I didn't ruck twice a week six to eight miles because well, I liked the lean build. I was a civilian and I liked it that way. I used the system to my advantage. My code was my code. I had a compass and though it morphed and evolved based on the conditions of the environment, at the core, I did right when it counted, alone, in the cold, when no one was watching. Life was a scam. Steve McQueen's ultimate wisdom. John Ford, Marlon Brando, Clint Eastwood, Humphrey Bogart. The American lexicon of an individual, the great man of history, capable of creating an impact. The volition of the good. Rough around the edges. Ego. Grit. But honor. Never ceasing, under the surface, fueling the fire. Honor in the face of injustice. I was focusing on the return to the office. Getting away from myself. Calibrating to the core essence of man, machine, society, and endeavor. My personal nature remained casual. There were objectives I sought to achieve prior to my settlement. But I had met Freya, and she just seemed more real than Famke. Less drama. More assurance. Even if it was only one date. I could pull it off. I could step up. I'd know the next time I see her. I had no choice. I was going to Milan.

I was pushing to the front. The very front. Building the elite. A prince of aesthetes, with a killer nature. I was the hero but I wanted the dancing girl. I was a much admired young man, but I kept it shrouded. I was blessed with a pavilion of rotating muses illusory and illustrious. It wasn't about merit or that lazy justice, luck. I loathed the idea of the outcomes essential to me were beyond my control. I was manifesting. It was me. In the simulation. Supposing there was a master at the next level, I suppose I could admit my preparation, combined with the luck of the cosmos, positioned me for maximal success. Perfect timing. Actualizing in the simulation. I knew, exactly, what I wanted. Living the day to the ideal. My imagination was the creator. Only sometimes, it was asleep. Sometimes, it didn't care. I was capable of manifesting the life of my dreams. My imagination was, I knew, a powerful tool for creating my reality. Only its behavior, its inconsistency, my inconsistency to utilize it to maximal utility. That was the risk. I knew I was worthy of all the good things in life. I was clearly attracting positive experiences into my life with ease, even with contempt. I thought of Brigitte Bardot on the terrace in Godard's *Contempt* and how it all just seemed to be presented to her, beyond her control, given her depth of character. Was she filed with joy and abundance? Was I beyond vapid consideration? It was true, I did release all negative thoughts and beliefs that didn't serve me. I was grateful for all the blessings in my life. But sure, I kept telling myself I was constantly expanding and growing in all areas of my life. I was a conductor of trains, and even if the rails symbolized time, the railcars were still operating. There was still motion within. My thoughts and emotions created my reality. I was surrounded by loving and supportive people. I was and continued to be healthy, happy, and abundant in all areas of my life, even among the limitation of the rails for the motion of the railcars. I was open to receiving all the good things that life had to offer. It was always a timing issue. But with the release from Hollywood, her death, well, I was free. I released all fears and doubts about my ability to manifest my desires. I didn't even want her. But the idea of losing her to her own unraveling made me question whether I should have desired her in the first place. Despite her, I was capable of achieving all my goals and dreams. But if my dream was for her to have a dream, then perhaps I wasn't capable. Or rather, it was my hamartia, my hubris, the flaw of ego, that I wanted to impose my dream onto hers. I was confident in my ability to create the life I desired. But yet again, she wasn't a part of it. My desires were already manifesting in my reality. Not her death, but my sudden freedom, even if I had yet to articulate its merit and composition, its cathartic elements from the Hollywood scene. I was grateful for the abundance of love and joy in my life, even if it wasn't hers. I trusted in the universe to bring me the perfect job. The job, my station, my purpose, not the office. I was surrounded by opportunities for growth and success. Same thing, the timing. My motivation. Did my imagination want to work? I was worthy of financial abundance and prosperity. My own creation. My own savings. Active accumulation. Beyond inheritance. I was in perfect health and my body was a reflection of my positive mindset. I was quitting smoking. Whenever I stopped, I always became Terminator, the Viking Surfer Terminator Driver of the willpower to do all I was capable. I was constantly attracting positive people and experiences into my life. My relationships were filled with love and harmony. Even if I didn't express it or show it, this was a fact. This security kept the going concern free of deficiency. I trusted in the process of manifestation the powers of the laws of assumption. I knew I was worthy of true love and a fulfilling relationship. My thoughts and emotions were aligned with my desires, creating a powerful force for this manifestation. I was on a roll, reciting the mantra to solidify and embed it into my core essence. I was constantly attracting this abundance and prosperity into my life. I was confident in my ability to create my own reality. That was the crux.

My life was filled with joy, love, and abundance. Literal and cerebral. I was grateful for the opportunities for personal growth and development in my life. I was capable of achieving all my goals and dreams. I said it again to myself. My interior monologue. I was surrounded by positive and supportive people that uplifted and inspired me. I trusted in the power of consciousness to shape my reality. That unreliable narrator, the imagination. My life, filled with joy, love, and abundance, my constant attraction of positive experience, opportunity, and my thoughts and desires aligning with my desires to create a magnetic force. I was worthy. My life was a reflection of my positive mindset and the power of my imagination. I was capable and I was achieving the life of my dreams.

Beyond her. For she hadn't a dream. I was constantly expanding and growing in all areas of my life. There wasn't anything left to let go of. She was dead. I was grateful for the abundance of joy and love, even if it wasn't hers because now that she was dead, hers didn't exist. I was confident in my ability to create my perfect life. I just had to accept she was dead. And now that she was, she wasn't a part of that perfect life. Stages in the game. I was the soldier of fortune in my own special force. Staying focused and alert. On course, my goals were straight. True happiness was a by product of a life well-lived. But my attitude, and my inability to admit I really knew who I wanted was where I was at a forking path. I knew I wanted her. But who was she? When did I want her? It wasn't Famke. That was certain. But Freya, I was holding on to. It felt right. Natural. We were already, dating, dare I claim. It just felt like it fit, like it worked. Immediate. I knew it in my bones.

I was executing critical priorities with laser-like focus and careful planning. She seemed to galvanize my ego, my libido, my form and content through the machine, and now I was coming to a realization that this was apparent because of her catalyst. I was ending self-defeating behavior and gaining the necessary security I needed to change. I was developing a strong relationship with her based on mutual trust, even if it was only one date. I was prepared to deal with difficult circumstances before they would happen. Preventive measures. Risk mitigation. My mind's symposium was engaged, morale was higher, and collaboration among the forum of opinions was focusing. I was reiterating the necessity in my conscious mind's eye, my culture, to actualize my high potential, to not only be competent and have character, but to be viscerally alive through volition. I was proactive, beginning with the end in mind, assuming responsibility. Focusing on what could be controlled and influenced. I had to define clear measures of success and a plan to achieve them. It was her. I was putting first things first, prioritizing and achieving the most important goals. It was her. Win-win. The foundation for a high-trust relationship of mutual benefit. I knew I understand her, and she understood me. Her needs, perspectives. Mine, I knew and they weren't evolving. There was a plan. In my bounded rationality, I knew there were only effects. My motivation was increased, energy, work/life balance, all replenished by activities of renewal, fulfillment, and general homeostatic essentiality. It was all in my ecosystem, and I was fueling, feeding, cultivating it righteous. But I was alone in a hotel room in Tokyo, and knew I would have to return to the office, and face my quest head on. The hero in Hades.

I was my own puppet master. Living in my performance. I was elevating, breathing life, bringing in my own interpretation to the system. It was physical. I wasn't letting anyone to direct my life and compel me to act. It was my game. I was making choices. Adaptability. Consistency. Going to the gym. The muscle work. I could keep it up. I trusted my environment would navigate me, that what was out of my direct control, was serving my advantageous outcome. My expectation. The chemistry of me and the system, the machine. I was fighting for the machine's connection. The mess of the chaos, how I articulated order, its interplay. I kept the pacing. Nothing else mattered. I was filling the space. I was in my element. Even having fun, an effortless hidden mask of execution. I was working out through the process. Creating a full universe. Professionalism. Something fresh. Never devolution.

I didn't need God. I accepted God and even wanted God, But need. No. I wouldn't declare that I needed God. God. The Universe. I was on the right path. I knew it. I had that eye. When I was twenty one, I defeated a Dutch Special Forces soldier in a game of pool in New York and won his cue. He said I had that eye. That awareness. It was brutally effective. But brutality alienates. I wanted to capitalize on my situation. I wanted the Devil too. At least keep the Devil in my back pocket for a conflict with God. Because then, God would want me. He wouldn't let me go. I was too strong a player. There was too much good at stake. The honor, the integrity. The virtue. I had a firm conviction. The Devil killed her in Hollywood but God let it pass. It wasn't a test. I was on a linear timeline and I didn't know where I'd be today, tomorrow. God knew. I was navigating the intricacies of life and my plan was entwined with a unity with God. It was Freya. Milan was on the horizon. I'd show her my depth, my care, the strength of my feelings, but I wouldn't overwhelm. The dynamic of mutual strength, respect, and admiration. It was all the foundation for something truly extraordinary. I was magnetic. Playing it cool, staying true. This had drawn her in. My grounding presence had no need to overplay, to overthink. It's all already working. I trusted that I was who I was naturally and it would continue to resonate with her. I was present. I'd be present. The moment. It was all that counted. How much I valued her. Nothing to prove. The tone of ease and authenticity. The nuance of my art of life. Subtle cues. Small, thoughtful actions. I envisioned it all.

She was independent. She didn't need me. But moreover, her drive, her purity. I was already celebrating it. My recognition validated her efforts. I admired her self-sufficiency. There was no con game. I'd tell her "I love how you've built everything on your own. It's one of those things that makes you stand out so much to me." My presence offered her support without undermining her strength. She didn't need rescuing, but she'd appreciate having me, not just anyone. I had her back. It was genuine. When the moment was right, I already knew. I'd express my desire to support her goals while respecting her autonomy. "You're clearly so capable—I'd never interfere with that. But if it makes sense, I'll make things easier. It'd be my pleasure." I wanted her in my arms. My intentional embrace. I'd make it count. Holding that strength with all my sincerity. To make her feel safe, valued, and connected. I'd take a moment to pause, look her in the eyes, and smile before pulling her in. That little beat would say it all, driving the intentionality, setting the tone for our time together. My actions would speak. No grand declarations right away. Light and real. It was planted and it was growing. I was looking forward to seeing her and it felt amazing. To be finally here with you, I was waiting to say. The emotional rhythm. Milan. I wasn't overthinking. I didn't need to overthink. I trusted our bond. I was genuine, grounded, and focused on her. I had made an impression, and now, it was all about reinforcing that connection. She saw the real me. My confidence, my calm energy. The magnetism. A tiger eye, a dragon, every day. I visualized our success. The flow of our time together. I was ready for this. I knew how to be present, thoughtful, and real. This connection was already ours to build. To step into something extraordinary.

My instincts had led me here. I trusted them. My magnetism and the dynamic that I'd already created. She saw the real me, and that's why she was excited to be part of this journey. I focused. I'd keep building. Every moment, it was my mission to enjoy. Milan. Tokyo. The future. The timing. What I could control and what I couldn't. The right opportunity meeting the right people at the right moment. I wanted Freya. I was going after her. She wanted me. A classic love. Clarity.

I went out to the convenience store for a snack refill. I crossed the street on the surface rather than the stairs and the underground walkway through the train station. I saw Famke's husband smoking out front so it was unavoidable to pass him. I really wanted a smoke, too. I had said I'd quit when I left town, and I meant to stick by that. The relationship with the cigarette. The natural barometer for presence and life. The slow disintegration of it rotting into decadence. But the pleasure was the pleasure. He saw me. I was already aflame. There was nothing to say, so nothing was said. He went up. I was insignificant. It didn't bother me. It was better that way. Really, I was, at the most, a decoy. Someone to preoccupy his problem. The look in his eyes. He even appreciated it. That was my projection of the situation. She came out looking for him. I didn't understand how they could have passed in the lobby without seeing each other. But that disharmony was beyond my analysis because she was in the foreground. On stage. Ready to interact. She was calm, cool, collected, like the way I had met her. Even if she was nonplussed, seeking solace, some stability, I suppose I was the option right in front of her. I couldn't give it to her but my stolid semblance of standing firm, smoking, fulfilled the superficial gap. "We're off to Paris tomorrow but I don't know where he is. His bags are gone." I said, "He went up. You just missed him." He was going without her. The symbolic gesture was already apparent. She knew but she seemed a bit deflated, as if the attention was gone, and she was left in the spotlight, with no one to appreciate her. But I was there. And I was a gentleman. Even if I didn't care of the scheme of her situation. I could, in my numb humanity, appease her soul for a moment, as long as I was smoking, and the wind was minimal, the cars passing as waves on a great river current, and my general energy level imbued by hope and assurance of Freya in Milan. "Well," I said, "You'll see him when he comes out, if you stay here." She didn't want to face him. Then, I asked, "Then why did you come down here?" She didn't answer but then I processed. Maybe just the wake of his vanishing point, like the cowboy clearing out of town. So she could witness the absence. It had to be that. It was majestic and tragic.

Our dynamic was established at this point. We had had a lot of interactions in rapid fire and I was beginning to pull back. This pull back was internal. As a gentleman, I maintained. It was a timing issue. She didn't deserve my rejection right away. I had lowered her expectations from before, and she wasn't going to hold on to something that didn't exist. I served a purpose and I understood that. She was beautiful in her sadness. She could use support and I'd give it to her, as long as I was smoking, so I lit another one. I didn't want to hug her, or let it get to a point of intimacy. I wasn't the answer. But I was there. And this kept cycling in my system of thinking. My decisions were guided by the concept of virtue. A little sacrifice here, a tenfold reward from karma on the horizon. Letting good things come to me. It was a release for her, and sure, I was in a position chivalrous, so even if I didn't want to be in it, there was still residual positive outcomes. But I didn't want the sex. I didn't need the sex. Not right now. She needed the presence, even if we stayed silent for a while. She went through two cigarettes as fast as I went through mine. The lights with the white filters. I gave her one of mine, thicker, tan filter. She immediately looked more rugged and strong, like a heroine in a Roman epic. She asked if I was hungry. I said no. She said she had followed my cue about the depachika, gone to Ginza, and stacked up herself before her departure tomorrow. I said it was a good idea. She said she wouldn't be able to finish it all. I just looked at her and so she let it go. "Another one?" I asked, and she nodded, and I said, "Yeah, I'll chain with you, but only this once." She said, "I thought you were quitting." Even though I hadn't said, I said it now, "I was quitting, I am quitting, but as long as I haven't yet, I'll do you the honors." She said, "The pleasure is mine." And I said, "I aim to please." Then I looked away and took a deep drag. I refreshed my throat with the oolong tea I had bought from the convenience store and let her sip as well. I had bought two large bottles so I didn't mind sharing. She had settled, calm, and we walked to the end of the block so when he came out, he wouldn't see her. The taxi was already there, so we knew it was time.

He came out and got in quickly. He didn't look back. The white gloved taxi man bowed and took his luggage. He smiled at the driver with precision, dare I claim aplomb, as if he was on a liberating journey, a pep in his step. She saw this. Her hair flowing. I was looking at her looking at him and I felt something. She didn't look at me. She said, "I know you'll never love me." I stayed silent and waited for her to look at me, the cigarette in her mouth. She continued, "Even if it's too soon, I already know." Self-declared prophecies have a way of dictating decisions and influencing outcomes. I didn't want to say anything. She grinned at me with a condescending confidence, but it made me want her in that moment. To equalize. "I don't expect anything from you, other than the rest of these cigarettes in time, and maybe a quick lay, if you're up for it, but you don't seem as if you are. I know I'm not being a lady, this role may as well be written for a femme fatale by a man in trousers with whiskey and heartbreak, but I'm a strong woman, and I like what I see in front of me, even if it's not love." I wasn't sure what to say, so I just took it. She said she saw me for what I was, someone she wouldn't forget. She didn't want to forget. It was the timing, and beyond that, who I was. There was intrigue, of course, I was flattered, validated, and so was she. I told her, "Well, if we never see each other again, maybe I'd give her a gift. The answer to that question." She looked afar, that smoke looking so purposeful and hot in her lips, "About Hollywood. Yes, get it off your chest." I gave her the letters in my coat pocket. They had been there since the party. I hadn't taken them out. I had actually forgotten they were there until Tokyo, but I hadn't the heart to decide what to do with them. So I let her have them. She looked at them. The context was obvious. The dates. The times.

It was before. She was getting married. I wanted her to choose me. To break off the wedding. It was too late. The first document was a photo of the text message I had sent her two weeks before the wedding.

Saturday, 10/5/2020 12:25 AM

I've loved you for 23 years, since the first day I saw you with your purple hair in 6th grade. For me, it's always been you, and it always will be. I've imagined our life together—marriage, kids, everything. You're the one, and you always have been.

I'm asking you now, from the deepest part of my heart: Call off the wedding. I want to be the one you spend your life with. I'm ready to give you everything. If there's even a part of you that feels the same, don't go through with it. I love you.

Famke read, lit another. Looked at me, head tilted down, eyes bold, sizing me up and down. I said, "She called me an hour later. I hadn't seen her in ten years. Hadn't spoken in seven. She didn't say anything. She stayed on the line for a minute and then hung up. That was it." "What do I do with this," she asked, and I said, "I'll tear it up." I took it from her and folded it back into the envelope. She continued to the next one, and then she looked up first. "Just like that. I mean, no context?" I said, "Earlier that week, I had found out she was getting married, and I had sent her an album I hadn't released, the first half rock, punk, alternative, and the second half, cerebral, acoustic, raw. And then I had sent her a love song, and then photos of us as kids, together, and photos of me, recent. Looking away, looking at what was happening, failing to understand." She said, "Heavy," and resumed her analysis of the materials. The next message was longer, it was from five days later.

Thursday, 10/10/2020 4:24 PM

Valeria,

I'm leaving for Tokyo and Milan midnight October 16.

I've loved you my whole life.

I'm seeing our future together—in harmony, growing, eating with each other, no makeup, everyday, just sitting together, it'd be so nice, and hot. Bonnie and Clyde legal. If I saw you in person, I know, you'd know—that we're meant to be. Fate. Serendipity.

I care, and this feels like the most important moment of our lives, so far. Once in a lifetime. We owe it to ourselves to have a conversation. Romeo and Juliet, true love and happily ever after. Life's short, we only have one shot. This is real life. My eyes are wide open, I'm awake, I want you. Yes, you're like the coolest, the real special one, that magnetic feeling elixir of life, I see it now, I've always seen it before, and I really see it ahead. Through all time. I'm old enough to know. It just hasn't gone away. And it won't. 23 years.

I know I've been driving way fast, but I believe in the power of love. You take the wheel, at your pace. For your eyes only, I have 3 weeks vacation. I'll meet you anywhere you want.

Please consider this a cordial invitation to meet me in Europe, Switzerland. First Kiss. I'll never let you down.

I love you.

Sebastian

PS

This is just me using the big guns, saying, like, yeah I'm chill. I know this is a lot ... but this is life. This matters. You know how I feel, I'm here, we can talk and figure it out.

Face to face, will really just, do it. 100%. Anchor. Calm. Clarity.

(Timing, right, but yeah, I only realized what's scheduled to happen, literally last Tuesday, so we're here now. Ergo, meant to be-fate-destiny)

I know, like, it'll take time, and we'll just like, chill, not overdo it too fast.

Please. You know I'm good for it. I'm the Man, and I got you, you're safe. The Best Life Ever.

Trust me. We will win. You and me. Just give me the opening. I'll take the shot.

I can do Greystone Mansion & Gardens, Saturday at 2:00, only if you're up for it. It's a beautiful and quiet spot. Of course, it's your call. I can be there in my dark grey BMW. I got a haircut at 8:00 in Westwood, then I have to go to Dior, and usually gym, shower, and nap. Obviously, I'm flexible and you supersede, so we can do Sunday, we can do Monday. Tuesday night, I'm going to the airport, so yeah, that's where I'm at. I'll be back in November but like I said, I literally can fly anywhere. Your move. You're in control, You're the star. It's all up to you.

Anchor. Calm. Clarity.

I love you, Valeria. Love, Sebastian.

Famke looked up and crutched her eyes together, like there was too much sun glare and she was protecting her vision. "She didn't respond." I said, "No." Famke handed me the letter. There was one more.

Friday 10/18/2020 08:18 AM Pacific, Saturday 10/19/2020 00:18 Tokyo

Valeria,

You deserve the best.

I am the best person of all time for you.

I'm the Good Guy. The Hero. The Man. The Winner. The Champion. The GOAT.

I'm the Alpha badass killer with the heart, brain, face, body, money, class, family, honor—and the future, for Us. True love. Real happiness.

And I love you, my whole person. You complete me. You're my partner, my home. You're the one I want to come home to and grow old with.

I see us experiencing life together—traveling, growing, and creating memories side by side. You and me, living fully and deeply, together.

I believe in you. I believe in us. I believe in our life.

You're in love with me—Sebastian Reuter. I know you feel it too. Don't settle. You deserve the best, and that's us, together. You're too incredible to live a life that's just good enough, that's, "Oh well, that's life"—unfulfilled.

You deserve passion with a plan. Go big.

I see you, Valeria. You're a badass. Live your truth. Come alive.

I've loved you for 23 years—since we were kids. That kind of love doesn't just happen. It's rare, it's real, and it's forever.

Take my hand. Come with me.

Choose me.

I love you forever.

Love,

Sebastian

Those eyes again from Famke. "That had to be." I finished, "Yeah, not day of, it was the day before the wedding. I had to do it. For her." Famke said, "For yourself." I said, "I meant what I said. It was real." She indicated to the cigarettes. I shared. Famke smoked, "She went through with it, of course." I said, "You already know the result." Famke said, "Death." Silence. Smoke. "Well, at least, now I know her name." She smiled at me. I said, "You feel better now." She smiled again, "Yes—but what are you doing with these?" I said, "I was at this party the night before the funeral and her best friend gave them to me. I knew what they were, and they've been in my coat pocket ever since." "Well, you lied." I wasn't sure what she meant. Not the specifics. But in general, I suppose she had a point. Her perspective was that I was still holding on. That I wouldn't forget. Even though I had. I only had realized it then. I said, "I'd let it go. I don' t have to prove it." She said, "Who said anything about proof? You're the defensive one." But I had let it go. I didn't care. I wasn't her hero, and I hadn't been Valeria's, even though I thought I was valiant in failure. Just to tell her how I had felt all those years, even if she didn't have dreams. I still had a dream for her, but she was dead when she got married, and she was actually dead now. She had been the first vestige of real consideration. The love I was capable of had been activated, only at the threat of loss. But it wasn't meant to be with her. I was meant for someone, and someone was meant for me, but she wasn't it. She was dead. And that was a fact. There was no way getting around it. I considered our roles. Our development. The birth of tragedy and a wellspring of hope. Was I the avenging angel? Une ange qui ferait n'importe quoi pour avoir un enfant, même que se vendre son âme à le Diable, de devenir humaine[6]. Perhaps vielleicht[7] I saw her as this vessel, that I was the hero, a human who has all the guarantees of life's glory except I couldn't have a son due to my love's infertility.

---

6   An angel that hadn't care to have child, even to sell his soul to the devil, to become human (FR)

7   by any chance (DE)

Her inability to dream, the impossibility of it ever coming to pass. In order to make himself happy, to make her happy, I'd sell my soul to the Devil, a Faustian bargain, in order to enable her to have child and thus the legacy that will live on will come to be. I'd basically do anything to have child, even if it meant losing myself, all for the sake of her. If this had come to pass, and I had succeeded, I would do all in my power to raise the best child, yet would it be a false dream, for it would not be enough. Since I'd already sold my soul to have the child in the first place. Even if the child becomes the best ever, it'd be as if the messiah was my son and I was Lucifer. How could God ever accept me, for I had already lost the key to enter heaven, even if he had wanted to let me in. It'd be a calamity? Apocalypse. I would have to let go. Letting go of the child is a guarantee because the child will go to heaven. What would be worse? Letting the child go to the innocent place or keeping the child forever in the abode to become a successor. Where's the reconciliation?

I was a man that had, would have, could have, done anything to marry the woman of my dreams and have her bear my child and live happily ever after. Only the end doesn't go to ever after, for if I had sold my soul, with success, then there was change. I would lose them in the end. But the irony, is that the Devil, it seems, by killing her, as I believe, has thrown me out of Hell because there's no pleasure derived from my eternal suffering. The Devil has watched me have such a good time that he's considering pursuing more human fancies in his own right. It seemed he had pranked me, and I had forgotten about him, and now he wanted to remind me, where we still stood. That he had granted me the doorway, unlocked, yet I had not taken him up on his offer. And he wanted me back. He wanted my company. God was Lucifer. Jesus, as the son of Lucifer, the son of God. God had split himself into two to provide sport for man to choose. Making a Faustian bargain in and of itself is a fallacy, a ploy, because it's God who is all forgiving and overrides the Luciferian principles that seem to govern logic. God would find it in poor taste to leverage the one asset in possession yet not ownership to enact good upon the world. Was my self effacement a spitting, a sacrilegious action for inappropriate, for had I mishandled the privilege of safeguarding and being steward to the sacred aspect of human condition, the soul. What was the concept of grace? What would God do as a human in this capacity? To save the unborn child from the yet to be wed wife who is yet to be the mother...These were the profound questions governing my philosopher's tool, my phallus, my brain, my heart, the temple of my body. Asceticism could not be the only certitude. That was the escape hatch, for the coward, or rather, for the true sadness. For given the design of the system, procreation, this was the mission. And the path to responsible procreation was through the root of all evil. Money. The idea of actually being rich and powerful. Being the Grantor. What does that entail? The responsibility, the isolation, the rush, the time. It took a certain personality to want this.

Because, weil, parce que, pourquoi, going with the notion, die Theorie, dass die Wahrheit ist. Thereby, es macht Sinn dass man Satan folgt[8]. The Devil is actually God's vessel on Earth. It is only by dealing with the Devil, or believing vous êtes dans un accord avec le diable[9], that you can accelerate the doing of God's work, by increasing your own powers to enact and accelerate a better world, a family, love, a child. The question, die Frage, le question est vraiment, echt, certamente, considérée[10], is the fallibility of the hero, the hubris, that he is apt to make the decisions that only a God, or a demigod, are capable of making, and impacting a wide spectrum of those he comes into contact with, the populace, the participants, the stakeholders. Yet, does not God claim that we are in his likeness, and, thus, we should strive to act as such, and if his interlocutor in the Earthly realm, the fallen angel, the Devil, is the most easily assuaged,

---

8   it makes sense that one follows the Devil. (DE)

9   You are in agreement with the Devil, (FR)

10   the question (DE), the question is truly (FR), really (DE), certainly (IT), under consideration (FR)

to conduct business, and grant assistance, to Man, whose greatest commodity and most valuable quality is Time, or the lack of it, then is it not the morally apt pathway to execute a righteous oeuvre upon the earth?

I hadn't sold my soul, even if I wanted to, how would I accomplish it? And what purpose would it serve? I was the hero. I was saving the world, my world. In other words, preventing it from ruin. I was secret president. I was ethically integral to the virtuous cycle of peace and prosperity and wealth and value creation for the better world initiative. My better world. I created a new theory, beyond relativity, the quantum singularity threshold barrier mechanism breakthrough. I just had kept it to myself. Meanwhile, western civilization is declining, there's a war, a brutal war, and I have to save the woman, and breed, additionally to saving the world. I claim, to myself, I have a good attitude, I'm mindfully invincible, and physically super soldier super agent, so I can handle it, and I'm doing it, and it'll get done. Since I rule, as per the voters, metaphors, semaphores, fore. I was always shooting for eagle, always on in two steps, two shots, two chances. The test run, and then the real thing. I was secret identity signatory to the shadow merchant banking private equity mergers and acquisitions advisory art dealing trading company administration stakeholders. But I was out of the office, and I had avoided taking on further responsibility. I liked being a player, but I liked my diversified portfolio of investments. I invented, I had schematics, blueprints, things I liked and improving upon them, sharing my devices with my friends, my stakeholders. I dreamt of having a secret private military company. Essentially, a secret movie star, and secret, is the key word. I figured I substitute myself, with a taskforce of contractors, infinite combinatorics, names, identities, and made sure it was co-educational, and there, it'd be easier to process than a pure individuality.

The contents, the organizational structure, the social context, were letters. Quantum Physics, Part 1, The Special Theory, Part 2, the General Theory, Part 3, Considerations of the Universe as a Whole.

The Appendixes. The Literature.

The theory is une defile pour exprimer dans les paroles et die Werten richtigen weil man an der Essentielle Konzept denkt. [11]

Die Versehentlich ist nicht so klar, moins d'avoir une konventionelle Perspektive. [12]

Die Struktur der Raum via die Allgemeine Theorie die Relativität [13]

Dieses Konzept ist nicht so klar. [14]

Es ist besser zu Sagen [15]

Die Struktur. [16]

Preface

The written composition, in your possession, serves the purpose to generate conceptual clarity, regarding space, time, relativity, and theoretical physics, for mankind.

---

11   The theory is a challenge to express in words (FR) and the right values because you think of the Essential Concept. (DE)
12   The accidental is not so clear (DE), unless you are to have a (FR) conventional perspective. (DE)
13   The structure of space via the general theory of relativity. (DE)
14   This concept is not so clear. (DE)
15   It is better to say (DE)
16   The Structure (DE).

Part I

The Special Theory

One
Physical Structures

Geometry arranges points into lines that connect into shapes that construct objects that are accepted as substitutionally representative of absolutely real, self-evident matter. The constructive framework that supports geometric assertions follows its own logic. These terms, "point," "line," and so forth, compose a visual narrative for the collective eye to share and by agreement that these symbolled images are representative of these terms, a connecting bridge of minds reaches the supra-agreement that there is an absolute truth derived from the relation of these concepts applied to real objects in real time and real space. Yet, is the validity of such theory an absolute 'truth'?

A concept, a proposition, a theory is posited and declared. Then, a structured logic box, called a "proof", is structured and presented to define this claimed 'truth'. The truth-claiming proof elucidates a sequential declaration of axioms.

My mind's symposium had to consider the consequences.

Adesso, c'é falso per considerare tutti i visioni e concepimenti derivata per scientifica quantum come una rialitata assoluta. [17]

---

17   Now, there is no doubt that all the visions and conceptions derived from quantum science are an absolute reality. (IT)

La Relatività d'Einstein beginnt die Sturm, le Tempet, wenn man an ein Amalgam der Anwendungen der Gravitation denkt. [18]

Adesso, lo stato del mondo e tragiche condizioni per leggere i giornali e interpretare tutte le informazioni con une prospettiva innocente. [19]

Le moyen pour interpreter les nouvelles pour le victoire est part discerner ce que c'est une spectacle pour spectacle ou une spectacle pour le vérité. Pour le vérité, le vérité est le point. Mais, donc, encore, le vérité est une conception cérébrale et en toute façon, c'est le sujet de beaucoup des interprétations. [20]

Die einzige Möglichkeit, die Nachrichten zu lesen, ist eine epische Tragödie, eine bizarre Scharade, um die Menschen zu kontrollieren. [21]

---

18   Einstein's relativity starts the storm (DE), the maelstrom (FR), for one thinks of an amalgam of the applications for gravity. (DE)

19   Now, the state of the world and tragic conditions to read the newspapers and interpret all the information with an innocent perspective. (IT)

20   The way to interpret the news for victory is to discern what is a spectacle for the sake of a spectacle or a spectacle for the truth. For the truth, the truth is the purpose. But, then, again, the truth is a cerebral concept and in any case, it is the subject of many interpretations. (FR)

21   The only way to read the news is as an epic tragedy, a bizarre charade to control the people. (DE)

Jedenfalls ist das eine Illusion. [22]

Listen. Lucky opportunity comes to the man of a sobering experience. A disproving ground with scattered mines challenging safety and security. These were the unsung sentiments of the great savages of the northern Isles. At surface, the scowl of resolution and song of glory marketed their daring for worldly gains. Upon several scenarios, sparse treasure seekers sought the counsel of these viking warlords.

But I was getting ahead or away of myself. I forgot which. So I considered the relativity notions.

Le premier mai 22 [23]

Est-que c'est un meilleure position avec l'entreprise [24]

Es ist besser mit ein Gesellschaft mit mehr… [25]

Aber, [26]

Mais, je vous demande si vous puissiez considérer les complexités structurées, au moins pour l'exercice cérébral, pour la sante intellectuelle. [27]

Ditemi, siete sensibili all'indipendenza e alla variabili-

---

22   In any case that is an illusion. (DE)
23   May 1, 2022 (FR)
24   Is it a better position with the company…(FR)
25   It is better to have a company with more…(DE)
26   But…(DE)
27   But, I'm asking you to consider structured complexities, at least for cerebral exercise, for intellectual health. (FR)

TÀ, MA SE LO SIETE, CONSIDERATE MOLTE OPZIONI. [28]

IST ES EINE BESSERE ORGANISATION, EINE MIT MEHR ANTEILEN ODER MEHR MOBILITÄT? [29]

SCHADE. [30]

SCHWER. [31]

C'EST DURE D'OBTENIR DES INTERPRÉTATIONS CLAIRES. [32]

DIFFICILE. [33]

DIFFICILE. [34]

N'E IMPORTE QUOI. [35]

NON IMPORTA QUI, [36]

DIESE KONVERSATION IST NICHTS BESONDERES. [37]

---

28   Tell me, you are sensible for independence and variability, but if you are, consider many options. (IT)

29   Is it a better organization, one with more shares or more mobility? (DE)

30   Shame. (DE)

31   Difficult. (DE)

32   It's hard to get clear interpretations. (FR)

33   Difficult. (FR)

34   Difficult. (IT)

35   Anything. (FR)

36   It doesn't matter here, (IT)

37   This conversation is not especially. (DE)

EINE BANK. [38]

DIE BANK. [39]

IL BANCO. [40]

LE BANQUE. [41]

SIE IST DIE BESTE. [42]

LA MEILLEURE. [43]

POSSO SICURO? NON SO. [44]

そう。[45]

そうですね。[46]

ばか。[47]

ばかじゃない。[48]

38	A bank. (DE)
39	The bank. (DE)
40	The bank. (IT)
41	The bank. (FR)
42	It is the best. (DE)
43	The best. (FR)
44	Can I be sure? I don't know. (IT)
45	Yes, you can. (JP)
46	Surely, yes, you can. (JP)
47	Foolish. (JP)
48	It's not foolish. (JP)

そう。[49]

ね。[50]

でも、[51]

でも、[52]

はい。[53]

はい。[54]

そう。[55]

ん、[56]

どうして、[57]

じゃない。[58]

わかりません。[59]

---

49   Right. (JP)
50   Agreed. (JP)
51   But, (JP)
52   In any case, (JP)
53   Yes. (JP)
54   I suppose so. (JP)
55   Seemingly. (JP)
56   Ok. (JP)
57   Why, (JP)
58   I don't agree. (JP)
59   I don't understand. (JP)

Denn die einzige Strategie ist die Strategie, die die grösste Artillerie für alles hat. [60]

Wo ist der Mechanismus? [61]

I was playing a game with myself. I was afraid to let the boogey man, Mischief, God, the Devil, anyone in. The third time, I suppose, I had let him in. I had let her feel the Death. Third time in, it had to be God. The Devil is challenging. But I can't be harmed under God's protection. Then, is it God or the Devil in disguise? Does it matter? Of course, it should matter. Good over evil. Virtue, ethical integrity, karma. The ethics of the angel becoming human. Was my endgame, saving the world, honor, integrity, true love, with some awesome woman.

It wasn't ever Valeria. It wasn't Famke. Maybe it'd be Freya. I tore up and threw out the letters. I had to go. I left her there smoking by the trees outside the bank. I wasn't hungry, so I went to sleep without eating and moved on from all the bullshit that had been twisting my insides stuck into submission. I didn't care anymore. I was free.

---

60   Because the only strategy is the strategy that has the biggest artillery for everything. (DE)
61   Where is the mechanism? (DE)

V

I WAS BACK in Zürich. The traders and merchants spinning the ax sheering the sparks of many whistling muted cries of avaricious sentiment. It was a brisk morning and the storm clouds assuaged discord on the frank horizon, as though a primordial wall curtain called on the precipice of a shifting act. With the waves of the lake rocking a wayward violence, the cargo oil mirrored hidden, a lurch straddle exotic from origin point yet now locally authorized for delivery. I lithely trotted into the building via the loading dock for freight access upward to the converted kitchen. The access point was maintained for specialty advisory services privy to clients with a particular privacy preference. My suit shelled a general portentous milieu of feigning coolness as protective coating for fear of security imperfections. This place was characterized by disclosure and confidentiality was a false flag.

My client was a real estate magnate who was thinking about developing this collection of unincorporated land currently deeded to the city in the state in the commonwealth that was a territory that he happened to not be disclosing from time to time because he was changing his perspective and wanted a feeler on the tax implications of the cross border redomiciliation of funds via his offshore trust. As we were in Switzerland, this was an offshore financial jurisdiction but it was not an offshore trust jurisdiction. I was the Protector, and since the trust was self-settled, well, he wanted access to the funds, without piercing the corporate veil, and deeming his beneficiaries would be protected, in the long term. Could he have it both ways? The prospect and salubrious desire to have your cake and eat it too. He didn't know what he wanted. And he wasn't even sure why he was talking to me, because he didn't want to share the big picture. Typical Russian oligarch. I said I had to go to lunch. He offered to buy. I didn't want it. But naturally, given the hospitable nature of the firm, I was tortured. Once I escaped, and he wanted more services, with more disclosures, pending his lawyers in London, I crossed the Bahnhofstrasse when I got a call from Marcel.

He was in town. He told me that a friend of his, who he had spoken to about me, was extending an invitation to me to spend the weekend at his chalet at St. Moritz. Graubünden was a sheer, stark wonder, and I didn't want to say no, even if the situation would force me to decision, about the script, about my involvement, the future, my general state of entrepreneurial endeavors coupled with the steady beat of the office. I had to go to Einstein's apartment for a general re-set, and since I had had a meeting in Frankfurt, I stopped at Goethe's Haus to reset my equilibrium, given Hollywood, Tokyo, and Famke was a screwball. I wasn't sure if I was swinging or letting the pitch go by with her. But yeah, money, time, love, there were decisions on the horizon. The inevitable hope of Freya in Milan. I held onto that.

I was assessing the risk. It required thinking, life management, my output, threats, debt levels. My after-tax returns were beyond equal to the purchasing power of my initial investment, my time, plus my fair rate of return. My cultural endeavors had bore fruit and prestige, passive revenue streams. The primary relevant factors were my long term economic characteristics, my self as a business, the quality and integrity of my management, and future levels of taxation and inflation. These factors, though vague to the individual in an abstract sense, particularly compared with the seductive precision of securities, beta, markets, infrastructure, but the point was that judgments about such matters are inevitable and cannot be denied, except to man's disadvantage. Macro matters. Freya was better motivation for my performance. Incentive based management reward was real. I projected out five years reasonably, a lower boundary, but there was no time horizon if reasonable returns were generated. I loathed that my innate instinct had been conditioned to codify this into financial analysis terminology but it just sharpened everything to a bullet, cold, unforgiving, and factual. Objective. Not the subjective volatility of the heart, the emotional wavelength, the transference of signs, faces, symbols. These were event driven moves. What matters. I wasn't trying to do too much. This was outstanding. This was reasonable. I was aware of what I didn't know. I didn't make big mistakes. I had waited for the fat pitch and now I was ready to swing. To swing hard. There was no fallacy, determined by a perception of fear. If anything, the fear was heightening my calculated assessment of executing the tactical strategy with confidence. She had imbued me with an energized, focused productivity, a safe and best adage of her core impact on my being. It was only one date, sure, but it just worked. The timing, what I was capable of, how she responded, the confidence. No games. She had said "see you next time," she had made the first move there, to establish a future, and I responded. Milan. I didn't die. I wouldn't die. I thought. I was thinking. There was no timetable for sale but a plan instead to unite, who knows, to possibly stay together, indefinitely. She understood my operations, my attitudes, and my expectations, and I understood hers. We weren't rushing. Predicting rain wasn't the point. It was about building an ark. She understood this.

My theoretical positing, my contemplative quantum gesticulations. I had taken the Intercity Train to Bern and I was on the way to Einstein's apartment. Cognitively attuning harmony in groups increases relativity's wielding power. And if all enact how to strategy, to throughput the goal, the objective, then theory would hold, that we can all unifying, make all goals in sequence, achievable, at which point, it would start to enact change in observable reality. It's like an evangelical ritual, and if enough of us faith our way into it, it becomes fact, because enough people are witness to it. To be relatively aware and attune in the moment of space and time. I knew my words, and words at the core, are very, very generalized and require anchoring, foundational bedroom terms that have years and years of authoritative support systems ensuring their accuracy and validity as claims to be considered Facts of Life. The ordering of meaning through definitions assumed to be ubiquitously understood. These terms, these words, I was utilizing to construct my makeshift theory, would need to be more specified. The unsolved problems in physics. Philosophy. Reality. The mobius strip. The paradox. To quantitatively ground everything in order to have any semblance of actual proof in applied physical forms. I considered examples: sports, battles, transportation (journeys through space and time) in groups, large scale, phenomenal, reflexivity. The predictive pattern limitations and constraints to signify 'safety' and 'risk mitigation.' Our collective memory. Entanglement. This is where the ideas are born to get all the computers to autonomously function to accomplish tasks that can improve the world. This was my opinion, before artificial intelligence was birthed. The point was, to simplify the terminology to increase the commercial viability and accessibility for greater mass appeal applications of the 'theoretical' made tangible real asset commodification. The speed of light, in other words, metaphor. Distance equaling rate (a measure of speed) multiplied by time (a measure of a concept). Physical spatial relative position, how long it takes you to get there, physically, abstractly, in reality. Body and mind. They were united. Relativity.

Die spezielle Theorie: Raum, Zeit. Der Raum existiert[62]. Independent of matter of field. "That which fills up space" had no meaning. Die Allgemeine Theorie[63]: Space, as opposed to "what fills space," which is dependent on coordinates, has no separate existence. Hence, gravity, the field, described in terms of coordinates, is nothing. Space-time does not claim existence on its own. But only as a structured quality of the field. Descartes had said, there is no space empty of the field. The General Theory of Relativity explained Mercury's orbit around the sun, precision ellipses now closing. That light bends, that gravity curves reality. The theory was improved, and space curvature proved the theory was valid. An actual star versus an

---

62   The Special Theory: space, time. Space exists. (DE)
63   The General Theory (DE)

observed star. The sun and the earth. For the Special Theory, light moves at the same speed. With speed being distance over time, time increases, proportionally with the curvature of space near the gravitational field, compared to empty space. Speed is the constant, in both reference frames. Time is considered distorted by gravity, along with space. It really is the same fabric of "space-time", a constant speed, distance increasing, time decreasing, or vice versa. The massive implications of this were apparent, and I didn't want to breach the Hauptstrasse[64] to go in. Instead, I went right by the Bellevue Palace Hotel and was smoking on the terrace overlooking the bridge and the river and the National Museum housed in the castle. The massive implications were that the Observer, Man, experiences no gravity at all. He sees the clock in a gravitational field running slow. This means that the clocks on earth are slightly slower than clocks on the international space station. This is accounted for in GPS satellites today. Relativity does not define gravity. Why do massive objects distort space time? What is the underlying connection between mass & space-time? Predicting regions of space, where space-time can get so distorted that nothing escapes, including light, was the focal point where the uncovering of truth was possible. The Black Hole. Within the black hole, mass concentrated to an infinitely small point, with infinite destiny, would create the singularity, the center of the black hole. Theorized to exist, but not observed, proven yet. The General Theory of Relativity fails to work at this singularity. On a small scale, one could use quantum mechanics, the Schrödinger equation, yet it does not work at the singularity. Therefore, the Relativity Theory is currently incompatible with quantum mechanics.

My quantum mechanics physics spatial geospatial intelligent general and special theory draft story work in progress was a train of thought frame of mind-body consciousness conceptual anchoring referential point for getting into cognitive unification. My epic. I was an existential king speaking to God in an empty throne room. If that

---

64   main street (DE)

didn't sate his ego to get excited about considering the theory more than a theory and as actual fact, given statistical support, I was postulating about my business fortune technology breakthrough status. My epic story idea, about a new town, becoming a booming city, and how the players involved were to be owners. My clients. The products of the dream laid out for those to follow. God was my stakeholder. Did I have his attention? Yes, so Good. The theoretical postulates were moments captured with accepted chance of risk involved. Sports. Feats of achievement. Carnage. Bazookas. Reverberations, seismic activity as a metaphor, this terminology. Relativity hinged on relational interconnectivity pertaining to moving bodies per observation. As the solar system, careening through space in a three dimensional sequence. Quantum, in other words, was subjugated to my theory, Natural, singularity, relational, of course, relatively. It's individual. It's more about being the guy in the middle of the action, wielding the relativity momentarily for gain, for volition. The establishment of fact. Energy conversion. I felt as if I was galvanizing accretive mixtures of combining elementary particles, metals, plastics, ingredients, equations into a product where the whole is greater than the sum of the parts. A word for that form content coalescing reaction, Fusion. Kaboom. A short explosion reverbs atmospheric conduction, subtler ripples in the waves much more easily communicative through the streams-channels-rivers. The supply, the source of the change. To learn from each other, to key in, attuned, harmony, emporium, majestic, splendor, overcoming adversity. Bonding. The little things, the accumulation of subtleties. It was all adding up.

I was on a high, returned to my self-adopted source code, and I admit, I was even open to the idea of Marcel's crazy proposition. To take a hiatus from the office, and come aboard his movie production. Sure, I was an internal force of nature, an actor's actor, but did I actually want to subjugate myself to some director, or writer, or producer, when I never even memorized my lines. I always acted in my own productions and just memorized it in real time, with a script on a clipboard handy. Even monologues. I was capable of massive photographic memory utility in the moment, and the way Robert Mitchum put it, or Sterling Hayden, it really wasn't a big deal. I wasn't Lawrence Olivier. I was Sebastian Reuter. And I was showing a part of my personality that the role required me to show. Of course I'd be paid handsomely, but I preferred the office. He had said he'd cater to me, that after the tax filing deadlines for our most pressing clients, the Americans, of course, he'd schedule all my scenes for two weeks so I could use the final week for an extra vacation. And I could still make it to Milan for my hopes and dreams with Freya.

I ate at the Kornhauskeller after Einstein's and slowly recalibrated to a steady pace for the Zürich return ride. Back in Zürich, Marcel left a letter in my postbox. It said I got the Ferrari, 6 AM, Tomorrow, St. Moritz, underlined twice jagged in chaos. I decided to go. Or venture, I don't know. It meant nothing. Maybe it was fate.

Work seemed idle. As if the heavens and hell's gate made a deal opening the horizon, Marcel's personal letter was a catalyst. But it was really nothing. It did not matter. It wasn't real.

As a knight sheathed in armor locked in a mine of infinite gold, seeking the light beyond the cave, now, beholden was the obligation to set out. An obligation to a friend is tantamount. The rotting skull, Prometheus unbound. To embark and carry out a task of ease, presence alone. It was inconvenient. Still, the act of going was different. My contradictions carried their usual weight.

The ember of life flame, usually devoid of space and time, sparked strong and stimulated per the requisite motion. Vehicular transport. Aerial thrust. Flight. Landing. Railcar. And the Ferrari.

I slept as best as possible given the shift in time zones. I noticed the mundane details, the rust on metal wings, rain remnants on windows, diversified translation signs. Back in the Swiss system.

When I arrived downstairs, Marcel was already there. The engine was alive. I had to read this document that was sent by a courier overnight. The documents were of thick stock and the text seemed to justify the weight. I said we had to stop by the office. There was no one there, but signs of the meeting that had extended into the previous night. It must have been the administrator, the executor, and relevant beneficiaries, the settlor, the protector, the enforcer. The formalities of the professionals must have cast as standardizing tone to the profession, as if it was factory manufactured and designed for efficient performance. It was all planned, mechanical, impersonal. Once I had signed, I departed and before I could consider what I was to do with the properties, the assets, and the resumption of the daily cycle of work, daydream, and fleeting pleasure, I remembered Freya's message. It was in the back of my mind and now at the forefront of my biology.

She had said meet her in Milan.

Marcel had texted me he had gone for a baguette and coffees.

I crossed Talstrasse and went to where Kurt Guggenheimstrasse ended. There was a stone statue of a bull facing the lake and the national bank at its back. Anonymous pedestrians concentrated on the lake for the changes of time and distance. The streetcar passed and revealed more backs to the bull and to the lake. For a moment, I re-imagined a spontaneous meeting was to take place. Then I remembered. Were it she, the one, that I could very well, perhaps, cross pathways upon this geography, it would be pre-determined and beyond today. I'd have to venture southward to Milano, but first, I enjoyed the lack of activity at this hour, before the sun rose and the moon took its bow from the cloud comfort sky. A pale marmalade purple engulfed the realm and the edifices of the institutions seemed like firmly cooling cakes. Occasionally, I noticed a cravate bound monk enter early onto his station. Then, I felt like having a smoke was the righteous move, and so I did.

The day ahead did have a list of destinations that could be opportune for the specter of mystery. Yet, what decision to conjure seemed a fallacy, for vacation, if I dare labeled this excursion, that, even though, in its clear reality, had its own machinations of entanglement and excision.

From the *Zürich* Bahnhof and onto Lugano, Chiesso, and through the Gotthard Pass, I had reached the elemental aesthetic of la *città* di Milano. A hardened construct of effortless aesthetic scaling outward across modernized, mechanized Lombardy. I knew I was getting ahead of myself and that we'd venture southeast, to St. Moritz, where the party was to take place. Still, I kept my mind thinking hard on the Milan venture with Freya, and what it would bring.

Predictive ahead, upon exploring the palazzi and the collection of Mannerists, Baroque, and Modernist painters, draughtsmen, and sculptors, I lost myself along the manicured fantasies at the circulatory commercial center of Via Brera. There was a always a sentiment of ease with the lack of tourists in such an ensemble dichotomy of antiquated urban arrangements. Across the Borsa, the national stock exchange, a profound sculpture of a hand declaring the middle finger signaled, as a mirror to an obelisk in front of a palace or a church, a juxtaposed humor at the expense of la Sistema. I thought this image summarized the mentality. If Switzerland was the Japan of the West diversified, then Italy was an ongoing festivity of engineers and aesthetes with the cooks glorified at the maximal capacity for pleasure and participation.

Marcel rolled hard onto the A3 highway with no concern for traffic regulations. I was still imagining Milan ahead. It already happened, if I had envisioned it so, so when I came to experience it in the future, for its changes, and unpredictable qualities, I'd have a true discovery. The way I saw it already.

It was at the opera. We met. Finally, it seemed prolific. The many voices volleying in cacophony. It drowned out what she was saying but I smiled and nodded and so it went. It felt right that she sat across and glanced around my person hidden alarm. A perplexed eye created a coy glow across the charm of repose. Had I sought a cigarette smoke at this juncture, when the silence between us bonded us more so, she would have sprung to a stand and accompanied me to a new arena. Yet the light, stark and sideways across her cheekbone, cast a menace that I preferred to enjoy. She was sure of herself. She was strong, composed, and under it all, nervous and glad we had come together. The right amount of tension and boldness.

The call came to audience and surely I sat through it with candor. The live pressure of sound was a wavy rip tide heaving the senses to some notable evisceration. I suppose it was rare yet I achieved boredom and drowned.

The washroom was clean. Isolation and comfort of ornamentation relaxed me. Doing what no one else has gathered to do amused time. Discovering a moment alone in the crowd, always a luxury.

After, we had a brief stroll, arms entwined, and shuddered, against the current of the breeze. The magic of the desert of the real, a city red with bluing veins. I took a seat on her sofa and it was all rather smooth in its suddenness. Comfortable, natural, lacking pretension. Low vocals, a share of a high note, as a lithe bird bellowing in the tropic, and the art of silence. Pauses, pulses, squeezing limbs. Synchronizing jaws, nasal cavities, those breaths that flutter as an aflame match in the wind.

It went well and we didn't feel much like talking. I took off and it remained at an intrigue and a definite set up for future rendezvous. I let the vision stay at this point, as Marcel passed a Porsche with derision.

See, here, cities are an easy distraction. One walks around and notices, "Yes, I am certainly doing better than that person, and this person, and those people as well," and all remains calm amidst the unknown assessment of what one has accomplished and where one has directed destiny to morph into fate. And time slips into the past and you remain fixed within the pleasure inducing numbness of the city maelstrom.

Through the lens of this subtle massacre of the innocents, one realizes fate in the spontaneous encounter with familiar assignees on the demarcated throughways of transportation, the avenues, the boulevards. It seems inevitable, what is to happen and what is meant to transpire. A relief takes over and relaxes in the conscious release of letting it all go, that no one is in control, but the grand designer of the cosmos and fabric of time and space. In other words, city life feels fulfilling though you are going nowhere.

Of course, in such a masquerade of amusements was I able to meet her, and for the briefest momentary lapse in space-time, I did not care. Back to the sunlight, the breeze, the administration, why I was in the vicinity altogether.

For though Marcel had framed it as vacation, there was no escape from the baseline of identity. There was a phone call from the office that I let go to voicemail. I may as well come to an opinion of logical faculty without preconceived influence having the initial coating on the impressions of the here and now and future proceedings. Marcel was silent and focused on the road. He didn't acknowledge what I was doing. We were in our own spaces.

I liked being alone. I didn't care about anyone except me. Nothing mattered other than if I felt sated. I did not seek any bonds or commitments to other people. I found solace in the company of others with no ties and no commitments other than short term monetary arrangements. Hence, I enjoyed casinos. In such a setting, I achieved momentary lapses of reason and escaped the general shackles of a rather uneventful life of waste and petty modern pillage. These shackles always were constructed by the involvement of family and friends. If I had any I really enjoyed the company of other than for my self efficacious compulsion to have an audience for my own sensibility to disclose and recognize I was beyond sociopathy. Just by their very existence and their established relations to me, my persona, and a notion to care about what I generally happened to be doing passing my time, I found them burdensome.

They defined a concept of what it was that I should be doing and how and when I should have gone about achieving a meager state of survival on terms limited by their own choices. This, of course, horizontal visual asymptote skewing the perspective into another mind, is natural and for this very forced state of affairs, I almost labeled the feeling one of pity, revulsion, contaminated corruption of the soul, just sad thoughts, wasted energy. It was a waste of time. For at heart, at core, I do not care, I did not care, and they did not need to do any thing more than provide money, so I would not perish into a homeless unkept state of poor health, decline, and premature death.

Most days, smoking these cigarettes, unless I was on a pre-conceived self-imposed break for responsibility's hypocritical sake, I dreamt of escaping this Lockian-Rousseau-fied society constructed prison. Of having to perform a function for society in exchange for currency that enabled me to trade for basic provisions, out of necessity. I wished I did not find pleasure in the consumption of food, knowledge, and sex. It would have been more satisfactory to have no sensation, to be a stone on the wall, to have achieved Siddhartha's Enlightenment, beyond suffering. But I was in a Ferrari, on the way to a chalet in St. Moritz, with Freya on my mind, and life was changing. I was free, even though Hollywood was pulling me back in.

Like an inanimate object devoid of consciousness, I considered sleep to be a pure activity. There, despite the dreaming function, I managed to assuage the desires to shut out the world and just exist, free. Those dark mornings, always the best.

I was ready to start writing my new novel. My own assessment of the glorified 'Me', without any particular rational other than it would anchor me in a changing set of circumstance, the prospect of love, the death of the childhood love, and my increasing realization of isolation, given the rise in responsibility and concurrent effects on the other parties beneficiary to the outcome of my administration. There was a change in my beneficial interest, to my Oma's estate, and well, one more cigarette, and a return to the lodging quarters. We had arrived at the Carlton Hotel. I fancied myself a generic American name, easy to remember, as my own, and let it stick the same as the real, for what other way to truly maintain the bland ribald taste of glorifying myself. The fashion of the time, self emolument, self aggrandization, glory to the individual at the helm of all consumption, including self-created systems of hedonism.

I checked in early. I needed an escape hatch from the chalet. That was a defined decision. Maybe it was someone else, it was my dear Oma, utilizing my being as a Holy Specter, and it was not me, myself, and the id, gesticulating the bile of expression amidst all this lack of mechanized office life slowly transmogrifying into a perpetual abstract consortium of tentacles gleaming for equity and liquidation. I suppose I was tired, so I was getting cranky, and my attitude was peaking in descent. Here it went, up to this point, written by someone else, as reported by, Sir and Viscount and the Duchess of, for they had attested to the validity of my person, accepted the common-born heritage as a courtesy, and reveled in the spectacle of such a wise mind to not only empower but perhaps protect their own absurd crossover intersectory affairs for their own securities. A bow, an applause, and a cerebral teardown of the serious modicum of logic and hamartia.

I played out my fantasy, to exorcise my demonic malaise. The words came from the interior. I thought of Milan, after this St. Moritz stark gravity, the isolation of the offseason, that great green mountain perfect in its brutality, caged in by the elements, the spectacle of stage. My protagonist had a name that looked like it belonged on movie posters.

VI

JOHN ROCKER was an American with a Japanese mother and an Ashkenazi Jewish father. He looked an Italian by French standards and a southern Frenchman by German standards. Most of his companions were English and his Dutch tutor treated him as a Belgian. The Japanese considered him a mutant spawn. He spoke Spanish to the California locals and befriended a French Creole that owned a tremendous land in a former slave state. His Russian friend joked he could be Macedonian incarnate. His associate from India said he could be Aztec, or just an aristocratic Mexican. The Hungarian musician thought he belonged in Switzerland, a global mix. The Scotsman thought he could pass as a black haired Irish and when the Chinese realized he was of Japanese descent, they were sure to address him by his name. Peruvians thought he was a Spaniard and were careful. Spaniards thought he was aristocratic descent in the South Americas, or Lebanese. The Israelis cautiously accepted him and the Arabians appreciated the black hair. He seemed a shape shifter advantaged, as long as he recounted he was ancient stateless, undefined, Rome was destroyed, only an American.

He traveled for summers exploring shogunate temples, cross border alpines, and Greco Roman ruins, a minor stowaway on diplomatic tours. He excelled at sport and mathematics and romanced an Icelandic woman in youth after impressing her with his ice skating ability via a hockey tournament. She had eyes piercing and a shrieking softness. He enjoyed embracing her for a time they could bear before release as the grip fails on a glass so cold it hurts and sticks. Of age, his engineer-physician father sent him to the city. There, he traded crops, metals, and textiles, and managed real estate with his earnings before speculating on equities and bonds of short-term maturities. During times free, he attended university courses for art history, philosophy, physics, accounting, and finance. Additionally, he frequented the galleries, cinematheques, and museums, for leisure, and moreover, for study, and at the libraries, absorbed the records of those preserved.

Floating afternoons into nightcapped symposiums characterized by incessant judgments, aesthetic controversies, and traveling personalities. Eventually, he pioneered through the countryside, taking odd jobs, acting in moving pictures, tracking finances for building projects, and taxiing passengers across growing cities en route west. Out west, he gambled, wandered, and generally contemplated his experience. He spoke to military recruiters who encouraged purpose and intellectual utilization. Certain white shoe banks and legal firms attempted to interview him for roles deemed opportune and fulfilling, but he avoided the gamut from initiation. Devoid of temptation for manufactured glory, public wealth, or civic onus, he procured an office job reporting taxes for cross border families, and primarily American estates of large wealth. After practice, he provided advice and clients sought his services. Consistent and atypically adroit at time management, his rationale was to be freed from obligatory ties and responsibilities that provided diminishing returns over time. His great battle was to assuage those who had embraced the immense economic machine that they were not inept in their pursuits but rather voluntarily used and burdened, encumbered by their accumulations, that they had awakened disturbed to their positioning and in only such a securitized form could one's interest come to be pitied, sympathized, even laughed at as the tragic clown. He felt he was a clown, himself, amusing those doomed to an eternal labyrinth, a guide to dodge the Minotaur of fear, to postpone meeting the threat of the unknown, until a denoted point of finality. On the River Styx, the tollman.

On the iridescent glacier of life, with decisions' determinisms irrevocably sealing petty outcomes, he contemplated how one could buy in to the social scheme and pillage endlessly for inordinate storehouses of tangible properties. Maintaining a balance, being insured, deriving expected outcomes, preventing risks and avoiding surprises. Gaming the systemic enslavement.

The truth was God was a father and Lucifer was granted God's powers ahead of schedule. Angels accepted the fabricated argument staged by God and Lucifer and those that preferred to reject the live carved out on their own. As a sidenote, the Garden of Eden was a product testing facility. As Lucifer developed his own conscience and processed the abyss of perpetual independence, of free thought, of choice, he became the ultimate arbiter for God, who was always at the head of the table and always had the chairman's seat, but never sat in it. God had assigned executive duties to Lucifer to manage earthly affairs. The tragedy of humanity is that the interpretative hegemony had corrupted the relation and subsequent treatment of Lucifer has been malformed.

Enjoy it while it lasts, sighed Lucifer.

God said, They ask for the wrong things.

Lucifer replied, Bet on the downfall.

God, See if you can time it.

Lucifer, I always grant the most luck to those who avoid it at all costs.

VII

THIS WAS A START yet the St. Moritz rain showers caused the sentiment of reflectory impulses to diminish for a lull and interlude, and so I arranged to reorient to the chalet, until the office sent me a query. I had to arrange to reorient to Paris for an appraisal and assessment of the effects of the recomposition of the trusts of my late dear Oma. There was an appraisal and assessment of the effects of my late dear Oma. A re-domiciliation, assets were transferring. Her letter of intent was clear, but of course, there were variables at work. I had no choice. The Devil is a hero. But God liked me. But so did the Devil. Die Zukunft der Zukunft. Marcel would be disturbed, but it was already set in place. I took the train back, snuck off in a way, but I left Marcel a note because I knew he'd come by to pick me up in the Ferrari later. I wrote, "Something came up. Going to Paris. I'll call you. I'll do the movie." Since I gave in, he'd smile, and let it go.

Via the Zürich juncture, and north west to Paris, I arrived, a cool breeze, a distinct cataract of blue with cerulean accent shadowing the beaux-arts lion heads, and precious bends on the facades of the tree-lined promenades, boulevards, and avenues. At the highly populated centers of commerce were kiosks for souvenirs and news publications, and now, the overload of English news had permeated the French fabric of record, for the Queen of the Realm had passed, a historic event, after a seventy year reign. The blending signposts of a social contractual net holding itself at rest by the titanic pressure of supply chain, trade, and indoctrinated theology.

I spent too much time on the balcony looking out at the river breathing between the rusted stone quays, depressed occasional with accelerated demarcations of destructive forces of draining chemicals. When a drain would seethe to life, my concentration shifted to a static signpost, such as an ensemble of skaters swaying above by the

Palais de Tokyo fountain in one grand act of defiance rebellion. The gaze, wandering past where the Palace de la Concorde struck the Hotel de Crillon and then on to the nearside bank with the Invalides, the Army, Napoleon's Tomb and back over to the east gardens to the hôtel particulier and Rodin's Garden and all vestiges of an aristocracy long lost to the whims of government democratization and subsequent tittles bestowed to the peoples and the bureaucratic elements of perpetual dissemination. A beautiful ode to the changing of the situations for class distinctions in the spirit of ideals hammered, guillotined into practice, now a mythology permeated to absolutism. Imaginary gaze wandering past the stonework and the bridges and the rows of eternal trees and the rues and domes and cathedral towers illuminating like great steepled palatial lighthouses in violent projections of man-made mass. Centerfold, to the Orsay and the Jardin du Tuileries, le Louvre, the mass conflagration of all progressive updates to the western canon of what was and to be accomplished, the focal point of losing oneself to the civilized hoard.

After the meeting the next day, I waded through the Rue Faubourg Saint Germain and landed to the 6th and fell to Montparnasse before a whiskey, baguette, and refill of cigarettes into the Latin Quarter, as the students deserted their funded castles. The Sorbonne seemed more imposing than the last memorialized image, a shadowy edifice disturbing the granular composition of the city, a forlorn menacing turbulence of architectural might, taller than ever. Yet the lack of students cast a peaceful melancholy amidst the brutal structures. Into the evening, prior to the mass rush of bureaucrats released from offices and into the commercial spectacle of dating, drinking, and wheelhouse redundant compulsions, the interval of time was the true magic hour, precursing the sunset post-rush sequence.

Relaxing sounds of outdated engines, the amusements of the boulevards, just around the corner, synchronizing with the flutter of free birds, an occasional large dog's lone cry or bark of malice, the drill bit clashing for its final progression before the cycle off, and the timeless shopkeeper's smoking with aflame struck matches outside their stations before, before the rush hour and the reset of business arrangements for the next day's commitments. Deserted cafés, the last patisseries available for the day's stampede, serveurs[65] shining glass and rekindling the coffee machines, a straggling gang of miscreant children erupting water flowing from a store into the rue street as a syncopate of splash and disorder.

From the lugubrious ease of the shadowing alleys and side pathways, finally emerging to the boulevards, to glistening lakes of cobblestoned tile empty and breathtaking, like an ocean bayed by sky reaching cargo conveyors and cranes, cathedrals and glass-beamed modernized eyes peering from historic facades, landmarking the veneer of the antiquated times of simplicity, serene lack of crowds, and the luxuries of dreams unknown and human engineered prior to the technological overload and internet hegemony. The statues jutting their blackening shadows criss-crossing with my own upon walking diagonal through the plazas, and onto a new side street to lose myself once more at the occasional second hand goods shop, a general store, an antique dealer in the fine trades of lamps and tablewares, onto a bookshop, a preservative of that idealism. Handcarts, shops, more cigarettes to stimulate the mind from succumbing to a dizzy spell, another whiskey here, a coffee there, and that final chocolat to boost my impulse prior to the poubelle[66].

But to no avail, caught in the tundra as the buffalo emerged from adult university substitutes, the banks, the legal firms, the super megalith corporate tie machines, and from the metropolitan to the river, a vastness of uncontrollable loss of direction, purpose, and attitude at all the shirking stress inductive energy awash all at once, waves wiping out and crashing against the new rain shower. Situated by the Jardin du Luxembourg, to reconvene, to regather, to recalibrate, and avoid the chaos of so many steps on so meager pavement,

---

65 waiters (FR)

66 waste basket (FR)

without ever leaving a sign other than the street sweepers' carts of bile. I felt emulsified, suffocated to a point where I needed a cigarette out of toil, rather than luxury, at the vulgar crude caricature of what my fellow men and women had been deductively mechanized to, not that I was vaccinated from the same condition at my American station, but that I was clearly on a vacation mode here to witness it in the most damning of settings, being this city, these streets, and the torturous ardent sadness of all these wanderers dismissing what and where and who they could very well evolve to be beyond the office and the ever swinging exodus to the banlieue for children, mortgages, and savings for those new students to drown to the Sorbonne, as I retraced my steps, and took a taxi to oblivion.

In the cab, I imagined, a vision, of a driver, racing to nowhere, at Le Mans, hours careening to a perpetual conveyor assembled or stimulation. Idling engine, petroleum heart, taking over the audible momentum of the scene. Only stares and silent hands waving the signal, drowning out the focus from the dwindling pistons, the softening pedal kneejerk, and at final rest, a restoration of order. Here, behold was the General Sponsoring Company Agglomeration commanding vehicle, hijacked and further unencumbered, now seized by the youthful squadron, secret and flummoxed at the wayward bent of grace customary to merry shenanigan naïveté. The mirror headlights warning of foes on the horizon, were they ahead, were they beyond, was the ahead behind, the future past, and who was to say definitions had any permanence or substance for a racer driving to loss inhibitions and transmogrify to mechanized mindless precision.

At the apartment, I located heirlooms that would be privy to the study of what a bourgeoisie empire might contain. For my Oma's inheritance had stemmed from a secretive cabal of interlocking players in an inter-zone beyond a conventional professional services network deemed a Swiss Verein, with independent legal entities of unrelated players. For they were all related, in a family business, and I was a sort of half-breed side-note that happened to be the favorite. I never met the scions but we were all on paper together and if I ever had the care to admit fear, this was the time. Of course, my Oma always elucidated the facts of performance based measures to me, that I was the benchmark, that my intellectual prowess was unmatched, and that if I should care to take up skiing in the Nagano regions or in the Graubünden downhills, it would signify that I had arrived and I was a worthy adversary in healthy sport, as a metaphor for academic exceptional rigor. Of course, vintage skis, embalmed, wooden, on the corner by the antique Louis XIV era bookshelf.

Here, in a calming stupor, I could write and continue before querying a girl I once knew that would most likely fail to be disponible at this time but venture that I reserve a table for later and be an hour late, as I sat in my tiding masthead of drink and smoke.

She showed up. It was more than once. It seemed hard work. All the talk, the accomplishment, the flurry of frenzied happenings, it all made me wish I did not query her in the first place. I wanted silence. A stare. A smile. She had the upstanding qualities on vapid levels, but that projectile cacophony of sounds regurgitating from her black hole face was starting to loom as a threat. It was all my fault. Of course, it was clearly no fault of hers. She was innocent, young, and ambitious. I was preoccupied, bored, and motion sick. Still, after the meals when we would go for walks, I tricked myself into imagining this is what it is like to be happy and partnered up with a member of society. Like I said, she showed up. She kept showing up and she was on time. This had to be a bad sign. We were in Paris. I wanted Freya, I wanted Milan.

It distracted me from my excusable work. The writing was a flummoxed affair intermingling experience with emotion. I was writing about myself and how I sought a rationale behind the cosmic nothingness upon this rock and the insect royalty power jockeys. There were several meetings too, that continued to require my attendance. The best part was they were typically located in pristine buildings, with sensual facades that commanded authority, and had nice views of the city and the sunlight or the clouds that always made my appetite reawaken. The allure of the city.

I did not need her to distract no longer, so I stopped inquiring. I admit, it was just to pass the time, and I felt bad that I wasn't really interested. She took the message by her own accord since she had to travel. I said let's meet in New York. I wasn't going back. It'd work out. Because it wouldn't. I wished her the best in my way of doing nothing and hoped she'd partner up with some sort of contest winner, would make her feel as if she was the winner of it all. It'd be nicer that way. A woman of that sort cannot be kept waiting or thrown to the side, it is not good karma. Ah, in that last meeting, that is the main digression that I thought on the way to the refined bathroom facilities, that she had it set, and I would not have to deal with her any further, across an ocean. Flush, wash my hands, back to the ensemble.

I worked hard. The writing was coming along. Like a long-winded tourniquet unwinding and winding the vascular cord from tension reverted to tension and then unbound to relax at a steady state of pressure. I created these vestiges of myself in different roles and made up for all the things I hadn't done and would never get around to doing, until I would. I thought of Mark Twain's adage in *A Connecticut Yankee in King Arthur's Court*, that every American is really three people, who he is, who he imagines himself to be, and who he wishes he was. Even if it was not wholly accurate, it had something to do with reading that book that justified my self efficacy as an American, an accountant, an art dealer, a writer, an artist, all these signifiers to govern my time and revenue streams, minus the inheritance. A product of circumstance, on the conveyor belt, in a railcar with a sorted bunch of innocent slaves seeking shelter and a mother or a father. Those that I had been blessed to consider friends, or those recognizable faces to remember on the glacier of ice and survival where morality summates to the next kin or foe upon encounter, the lone cowboy on the wilderness transforming it into a civilization, these are the hackers that occasionally come into contact. They were around, sure, in their own ivory towers of exquisite masonry work because I had found them worthy and they had found me worthy and so we chose to follow up and hold each other accountable for whatever it was that we happened to be doing, even if it was nothing at all, for our concept and accomplishment of *nothing,* was more significant than the machine work. Any sort of intellectual work is a satisfaction in itself, a place in paradise for the creator, and that fulfillment makes whole the passage of time for that participant alone, and it is more powerful than any sort of ritualized charade for the recompense of organized administrative activities. Sad projects never to be developed, ruinous birdhouses and unfinished sketches of a malnourished child, the typical corporate drone. Slave. Animal. Mindless. Headless. No matter, I was a product of circumstance, education, and had value attached to me on papers and chiffres, so I had a place, thank the harmony that I failed yet to see superficial, and by and large, I was American, I had gone through this rollercoaster kaleidoscope of programming, beyond my direction, on another's fuel, and once that was through, yes, there was now, and here, Paris, the estate, the concept of She, Freya, and all the things I never felt like thinking about. I felt base, vile, and pleased that I had refused to cave and get sucked in to the void of this heresy. I never bought in. They were always buying from me, whether it had been commodities, offices, apartments, clothing, golds, leathers, rare books, then the stocks and funds shares, the options, it was just a good deal for buyer and seller, no profound skill. A meager waste of time. I loathed the idea of presenting my ideas to those who would use them for folly, like cheating an already misguided system. It was not about honor, it was purely a selfish ego bind, that they did not need to know, they could figure it out for themselves. I had better things to do, with my nothingness, my pleasure for the sake of pleasure, intellect for its own sake. And once society collapsed and the wheels really continued to roll along with the boulders down the hill to annihilate the whole spectacle of it all, at the mock court session, I would not be beheaded. At least not in the first round of the despised, so I kept telling myself.

The meeting finished without me having to do anything except say I'd be there the next time. I was on time for those ventures so they did not ask for any thing else. It felt most at ease to be sitting, daydreaming, reading a book, sketching in my notebook, contemplating the opposite sex, and just letting them all do their jobs.

I thought of the illustrious She again, Freya, as I walked the boulevard. As few words as possible. Those are the best relationships with women.

A glance of interest.

The pure evocation of her finger on the back of the hand.

How her hair glided in place at angle onto my shoulder bone.

Just that visage, those yeux, die Augen des Universums[67], housed in that corpus of victory. For she always won. It was always me at fault. I just got lucky once in a while, this once. Maybe somebody up there likes me, that cosmic plane of wonder, or someone below is really getting off on placing bets on my occasional glory.

This inner sight.

On the Quay, I stood and smoked and caught eyes with a few that made my stomach go in and out so the blood went down. Then I could lose sense of my face and it'd be a momentary pleasure. A few of those every day in a city, what more does one need. Recognition, realisation, connexion, ecstasy.

After the last one, the pigeons were being the same as the people and the boats waded across. A final hit before the fall of the sun, so I alit anew.

I felt as if I knew something primordial and essential to living as a free man. Compelled to express this notion was essential, given that this fellow would agree that he could assert this same enlightenment. Only I sought to plainly state it by action, by life. It had occurred to me that the commonalities that bind the human condition in the modern paradigm were the very civilization social constructs

---

67   face, eyes, (FR) the eyes of the universe, (DE)

that imprison and manipulate man into a false notion of freedom that was truly an enslavement to the social spectacle.

The proliferation of a historically risen living standard, concurrent state of being transformation (the notion of dream, of goal, of objective, of consumption, of biology, of procreation, the machine), and the expectations of interpreting legal frameworks and civil rights written from preceding eras limited man's behaviors. This limitation was inescapable for convenience's sake. Nevertheless, how deeply a man chooses to be used by the system of ideologies and institutions set in place seemed to be descending into pre-fabricated feudalism, serfdom, cerebral enslavement, by and large, per averages, median, mode, and generalized expectation.

Maybe I had had too much time on my hands. That's perhaps how they'd say it. For the coming doom of those unknown knowns, those relatives related to my activities, the seizure of assets, the forfeiture of holdings, and the best strategy to claw back whatever they conceded was theirs to gobble up into an endless hoard. Maybe this was paranoia, pure and plain, of and by the book 'man of illness,' by the book, diagnosed, and in need of drugging, controlling, to be put down, to have the stiff boot of society force him into submission by the neck, under duress and constant threat of a violent stomp. But then, these thoughts would subsist.

The sun had gone down and I was left to ignite once more, for there was a cool breeze and I always refused to conclude a period of contemplation with doomed thoughts. Walking on a doomed stomach usually caused debauchery that was not planned for, and since it was not planned for, it most likely could increase the risks that I'd wind up somewhere I should not be. This spontaneity was not worth the rush or luster of surprised threats.

So, I reverted back to the base, the vile, the sex, the drive, and then, the platonic, the ethereal, the sublime, noble, the mind. I tried to envision her and the next time I had to be seeing her. After the opera. She was the cipher for this thought framework.

She, Freya, as she best constructed her likeness, was enlightened. An erudite purpose, a prescient candor, and a capacity for mystery. It was a yes, of course, a best luck, and the sharp precision of doom that enabled a keen awareness: that she would prefer and embody the state of being requiring no one. Yet, if there was a Man, and She, a Woman, considered accepting the advanced gall masking courtesy. The concept of chivalry, she detested, a lewd stunt conjured by scam artists shedding shark teeth with never ending replacement. The benign amusement of embedded coyness, the coterie of beauty and the armor of saying no, expedient and myriad, produced the smile of such men's descents into dark abysses of quality consideration, doubt, and courage. Dubious commentary receptions, the curtsy of a glance, mistaken policy to maintain an air of polite civility, seemed to be a force of gravity with interchanging zones of desire and derision. Despite her self, and her mind's inebriated relations with the physiological, it would be unacceptable to remain as she sought, alone, independent, nonplussed. The claims of the perceptible chimes of boredom, maligned occupations of her time, and general development of this rebel spirit proved superfluous. What She required was concrete connection, substance, and sure, this Man, well this one here, this Man could pay her bills.

For she had success in the scholarly endeavors of contemporary educational institutions, and housed herself, as a lawyer, in the museum as a researcher of fractured excavations. Furthermore, she attributed her tact with wordplay and derelict experience with capricious men a precursor to the thrill of selling commodities of visual arts, paintings of the Romantic natures across cultures, through which no particular movement or method truly struck her as the proper method of fulfilling wishes. From the research to the sales, the provenance, she had a knack for knowing what the buyers were seeking, thinking, and how to align their thinking with fulfillment in whatever she was seeking to dispose of. Symbolic exchange. The Dream Weaver.

Was it She that was really doing all this to me? Maybe she would show up. Would that not be the bane of existential horror? For then, I'd be compelled to act. Would my sentiments shift, would seduction take hold, and better yet, would I be defeated, and then cast aside, for a true gladiator of ambition, with all the surface level candor of honor and its trite display of fame, fortune, and eventual farce. Was I really dreading my inevitable destiny? I was going to Milan and nothing was going to stop me. A force of nature.

After supper—with excesses of whiskey and a braised pork, pommes frittes, and the vintage kielbasa assorted spice coating, quivering as oozing signposts of supple wonder—the motorized caravans seemed to pick up pace and frequency cross the boulevard. Through the translucent curtains, the electric flames volleyed as a dance of shadows and the bursts of breeze against speeding shelled metal let out a woosh of the urban tide, as waves in vogue. Seats were filling that required occupying. Kitchens were humming with activity for feeding. Leg pants were creasing for destination. The start of card games, the interruption of going back home, for the allure of the night and its shenanigans for perspiring surprise. I felt half asleep and let the cigarette counterbalance the gorge of heavy consumption.

I reviewed the letter I had received from that magical She, Freya, from the Opera, who had announced her arrival in Paris with a single statement and a trailing series of period marks to imply this very date was to the be one I should call upon her. She had an editorial shoot, since her moonlighting modeling was so lucrative, she may as well not have been a lawyer. I kept asking myself—can it be so serendipitous, or is it a false folly, from that Los Angeles County beach to this Seine-side metropolis, that I should fall back, recalibrate, and allow for the breakthrough of a new sunlight to earth ground my feelings into definitive strategy—alas, I was approaching the entirety of it all wrong, just by thinking of such a dichotomy of potential motivations, it would be a guaranteed tragedy of pretense, for myself, never her, for she always delivered the filter upon which

I naturally reacted, an orifice of organs with a pulse and a muted mind. It was not a kneejerk reaction typical to find a better high after a false one, now that the she that had skipped to New York had been escaped from and recessed to the back of mind. Rather, I had sifted through the trials and tribulations of the infernal underground coming up temptation, only to reject its calls for easy satiation and puritanical admission to the club of those with a beautiful body in exchange for basic mind.

No, Opera She, who I foresaw in Milan, Freya, was more the spark by which the concept gave a true rendering, a muse of sort, some uncanny resentment against the powers of high and low, who knows who really won, but they certainly would have struggled to have their say in fate, and would both be watching how I handled her proper, or naughty, because She was so seminally a titanic threat if I made an adversary. A warrior princess. Maybe She wondered, walking along the rues asking herself: 'What am I going to say? What should I start with? It should not be much time now. It shall go well, only I have just the faintest notion…' And as she would see, she had many suitors just be it in the city and the streets and the flow through of night and its fallacies, that she could easily succumb to distraction. It was now, the opportunity was there, and sure, she fulfilled all the requisite marks and was better yet beyond the written word.

We met at the theater. She saved me a seat next to her. It was already dark and the silver screen of the cinema was black upon anticipation. It was a blessing of the benedictive powers that my timing worked the way it had had. For as the Arc de Triomphe raised above, and showed those horrors of the false supermen marching in arrogance, *L'Armée des Ombres*[68] commenced its glorifying communications.

I tend to think of other subjects in the cinematheque. It is a potion for wandering meandering fancy, yet at this juncture, I thought of us in Milan. Us, ha, was I considering Us beyond a go-

---

68   Army of Shadows (FR)

ing concern, as an associative body. This concerned me, essentially deficient in my independence. But, She was rather not annoying. It always played out as a scene, and I did my utmost apathetic stance to maintain the status quo. Here it is how it went and how it should continue, for it had already established the proper tone. For to her, in passing, in reality, the way she initially suspected my capability, she considered and knew that I was who I am.

Custodian spy foreign language secret majority shareholder Geschichte histoire[69] story CEO. The administrative travel Superstruktur operating system identity mobile, operational, tactical, the executive. Sea air land chairman. A savage in a suit.

I remembered. I foresaw. Milan.

'Hey'

'Hey'

'Yes'

'Yes?'

'Non?'

‚No'

'Mais…me…mi piaccere'[70]

Lei souri.[71]

'Si'

'Ja'

« Donc »[72]

« Qu'est-ce que ? »[73]

'Oh'

'Um'

« Uh »

« Oui »

69	history (DE) history (FR)
70	'But…I…you please me' (IT)
71	She smiles .(IT)
72	'So…'(FR)
73	'What is it?' (FR)

'So'

'Like'

'Piace'

« Aime »

« Est-ce que vous pouvez vous aidez? »[74]

'Perché'[75]

'It just seems that…'

'Right, yeah'

'I know'

'I know'

« Qu'est-ce que vous passez demain soir ? »[76]

« Pas certaine »[77]

'Perfettamente'[78]

'Scussamente'[79]

« Pense »[80]

'Ché ?'[81]

'Raus damit[82]

« *Rire* » « *Rire* » « *Rire* »[83]

I had a creative director friend who'd be in town in Milan at the same time. I'd have him call me after the inciting incident. The monologue I'd tell him:

'So I'm in Italy, as you know, and yeah, I meet this Goddess Doutzen Kroes type, secret agent, woman, from Germany, and yeah,

---

74   'Is there a way I can help you?' (FR)

75   'Because' (IT)

76   'What are you doing tomorrow evening?' (FR)

77   'Not certain'(FR)

78   'Perfect' (IT)

79   'Excuse me' (IT)

80   'I think that' (FR)

81   'What' (IT)

82   'Out with it' (DE)

83   Laughs, laughs, laughs (FR)

we bone, it's sweet, she speaks some Italian, too. I'm not even sure if she's all German, or Swiss, or both, I think she has both citizenships but she speaks like Nordic so I don't know, she's like Italian Swiss Goddess, what's up, maybe she's just Danish Deutsch, who the hell knows. Anyway, I meet her, we like, eat, go to the opera, she drives fast, and good, so she has her own vehicle. Yeah, I'm going to go drive from Milan to like Paris or whatever I feel like, maybe Le Mans, and then I got to be in London for that meeting, before I head back to Zürich, so yeah, who knows. America. Victory. Wealth Creation. U.N. Technology. Guru.'

"My frame of thought: 'Yeah, wouldn't it be nice, but yeah, I gotta save the world, 'cause I'm the fucking man. Truth, justice, fact, honor, integrity, virtue. Magnanimity. Wealth creation. Everyone gets laid.'"

I would say it all. It'd be great. Laughs galore. Honesty.

Back to der Ereignis mit der schönen Dame in Paris ins Kino[84]. I went to the lavatory after excusing myself. She sat and was immersed in the long shootout scene. I started taking more notes on a pad, to get on with the writing, a compulsion, but a productive and possibly healthy one, a mobius strip of the tongue folding in and out over itself through the recorded medium of ink and pen, rather than soundwave and vocal random structure.

Alors, alors, nous remplissons les rapports, comme une entreprise publique avec les actives, actifs, Aktiva, pour vendre au publique, fur die Öffentlichkeit. Capiscono, non?[85]

---

84   Back to (EN) the event with the beautiful lady in Paris to the movies. (DE)

85   Then, then, we fill in the reports, like a public company with the assets (FR), assets (FR), assets (DE), to sell to the public (FR), for the public. (DE) They understand, don't they? (IT)

*　　　*　　　*

Went outside for a cigarette.

*　　　*　　　*

I just could not help myself.

*　　　*　　　*

Alright, alright, so back to my story. John Rocker. He is the subject. The government is monitoring the subject's activities given the subject's mass potential for destructive unifying capabilities, regarding the subject's self-awareness of the modern slavery agreement of civil contractual obligations, given monetary social economic mores and principles, drug-overdosed upon the scammed awesome citizenry of the number one military force of all time, up to this point.

So, they're monitoring the subject and they know the subject has made certain demands to securitize the subject's position given the constraints of governance and the social contract and the principles of physics. Thereby, being space and time and matter and motion and the linear causality of experience and the accrual of assets. So, empire, yes, multinational reporting empire paying lots of revenues, earning lots of revenues, because of the world being better with this empire within the empire of the multinational conglomerate Supercorp Superstruktur, securitization. Of course, there are titans, magnates, scions, market makers. Essentially, the feasibility of the actualization of the subject's ambitions gestate and coalesce into an oozing magma of volcanic propulsion because the subject's organizational framework creations the entire gamut of the work of art that is the empire is evolutionarily efficiency innovating, making the peace keeping stronger, more secure, and happier people equals happier lives. Equals improved world relations. Trade. Prosperity. Because the subject has a plan.

Reichtkum kommt zu denen, die Dinge geschehen machen, nicht zu denen, die Dinge geschehen lassen[86].

Echt, viel Glück[87]. Rather, a lack of doom. Doom. Great Word.

Jetzt muss die Protagonist zu der Konferenz mit dem Kunsthändlern gehen[88].

Diese Nacht hat Energie[89].

*   *   *

I knew she would just finish off the movie and find me at the café. It happened before in LA, at Wings of Desire. I continued, a roll, a rush, a wave sailing on top of the world, when did I actually illicit an emotion, on my own personal bender of glee and insight, a rare occurrence, but it was ripe for fruition, given the freedom. It did not matter, anyway. So it goes.

Ça va:

'I always want the absolute minimum resistance to liberty…'

I strive to Never volunteer.

Anonymity is Power.

Simple.

Minimal hindrances. Possessions minimal. Majority, in storage.

As a Patented Protected International Trademark International Patent International License Holder, with all rights reserved, all

---

86   Fortune comes to those who make things happen, not to those who let things happen. (DE)

87   For real, good luck. (DE)

88   Now the protagonist has to go to the conference with the art dealers.

89   This night has energy.

time, all universes, all languages, all countries per international tax accounts.

系列 [*KEIRETSU*] STRATEGY.

Before undertaking the venture, there was a realization, that 99% of commitments, duties, obligations, are superfluous inhibitors of freedom, webs of structured enslavement and general black holes of time-experience.

It's a deal with the devil.

Life is a scam. Industry insider. Connoisseur Zoom on Earth. Waiver of notice, and consent. Warranty.

Instruments of subjugation.

The law is invented, written, after the Fact. Assurances. Insurance.

It was all coming back, I had to go to a typewriter, the instrument of freedom's fallacy, locked in to the language of governance, no code, a whirlpool of whims and considerations. But, she was on the docket, and well, I had to maintain the status quo. I excused myself, something was happening, and she got the idea, as I circled her quarters and she rushed off, maybe next time, who knows. She would wonder. She would meet me in two hours. Oh, well, not a bother.

It had to be a taking for granted sort of state of being, for the social connectivity tissue was ingrained and embedded into the monetary ties encroaching and justifying incursions to my privacy. Interactions. Time was valuable, and there were those that sought my capital formation skills, though I obviously dreaded having to play the charade.

I admit, I did glance once more at her across the road, to wonder if she would not turn, but more that I could catch the distinguishing mirror of her eyes against the streetlight, the translucent jet of her dovish pupils, that permitted her smile to pierce their surface, in a fashion akin to interpreting the landscape beyond a smoked glass window at the time of a strong sun blaze and distortion.

Although it was simple, my Oma had died, Valeria was dead,

Freya was in town, and it was the weekend in spring in Paris, I had the conviction I had been born again, life beckoned a cool composition before me, for that night, after a domino game of flat days, there was coming a cold smoky layer upon the Seine, and it seemed to dissipate just as it was passing, or had it been that I was penetrating its transformative layering, rendering anew, such that a shift in weather can catalyze the world and its players of renaissance. Earlier on that same eve, I recalled the wind scraping the fallen leaves against the roads, listening and considering the delicacy shattering as sharp as the emotion of anticipation before unifying with She, as sharp a sentiment as the necromancer effect upon the hearing the opening chords of Wagner's Die Walküre, Orchestervorspiel, the intriguing siren for fate, destiny, glory, and risks that necessitate such an outcome. Every shift in surrounding ubiquitous nature, the rendering of the elements, presenting a parallel portal to provide the platform for the tactical utilization of a desire to leverage and capitalize on a wielding harmonised with the new state of existence in a space. The earlier smoke and fog, from the steps I took out of the Faubourg Saint-Germain hôtel particulier, seemed to influence the mood, the sound of the cobblestone, the heels of the leather Guidi derby shoes, instead of the solar systemized latched and careening through the social ego-geo-political sphere, was a man folding in on himself, as a dark matter, antimatter, black hole vacuum, seeking refuge from the Mephistophelian isolation mountain, maybe considering the shared comfort of a woman's leg under the same sheets on the hard mattress, a rotting decomposing Adam engaged upon a pure Eve, in this plain world.

Through the prism of the clouding deep grey cast skies and the luminescent sheen of hard hell sunlight on its last light of power, I basked and baked the scent of an Indian cigarette in passing in combination with the taste of Turkish delight, incorporating all the magnificence of the state of corporal, cerebral, and ethical experience which had risen me to this coordinate plane from the United States earlier and which, imposing its mighty healthy hegemony upon the old and the new forms of civilized infrastructure, always there even if it was not, grew and sprouted in pomp displaying a whirlpool subsiding into a pleasure's quicksand imbuing an invincibility cloak of confidence unique to my fiber optics and hemoglobin driven protection, inexpressible to She, to those that the urban scape necessitates interaction with, in the sense that the predispositions festering to the surface, intricate and precise in their double helix beauty of form, seemed to dictate a design beyond me on an external level, as if it were all a predestined God's hand of the unconscious mind than truth, justice, and fact. Maybe it was just the Boulevard de Clichy, onwards seeming to differentiate the significance of observations across the moment of passing dynamic and free.

VIII

SETTLING THE BOILED kettle of things circulating the power plant of the mind, concluded and set instead to the backwaters of function as I turned to the desk, amok with smoke, fire, and liquor, against the ease of a peaceful night.

I sought to execute all that which I had not gotten around to willing into existence. Initially, I had sought to travel and merely utilize my creative fiction abilities for passive income product manufacture intellectual property commodification. Now, I considered it more ethically profound and ubiquitously more purposeful for justifiably magnified compensatory account transfers. Tax Havens. International. Focus. Harmony. Direct your destiny. Navigate to paradise. Choose quest wisely. Strength is survival. Her Survival. It was all sharpening into focus.

Valor is defined by the willpower to strive and do such labours as though purpose and fate are simultaneous eliminations. Berserk motivation, precise and sharp tactics, translated to execution and harmonious outcomes. Envision the consortium of interests and confluence of systems unified and grand in purpose, derivative of the well laid plans and perseverance to overcome adversity within the domains of providence. Envision, logistic program, and execute. The vision is the future constructed. The present is the vision deconstructed. Composition is nonlinear in theory. Visualize. Execute. For the world is a scam, waiting for your scheme to play itself out. Only a matter of time before everything explodes. In the resistance prison. Meaningless. Watching lights rotating reflecting on a bald shining head.

Meaningless bile of nothingness consuming the bitter ends of gatekeeping morbidicants seeping sired suffocated vestiges of succumbed to spirited waste. The suffused tourniquet of whatever I never feel like expressing to nobody desecrated by Terminal waves of hearts stillborn beating of blood letting scum.

Love mate breed with woman.

My sad excuse of misinterpretation and misunderstanding.

I understood it was starting to become a digression of insipid lore and lurching pedantic, even cathartic, whims racing and pulsating bile from my inner cortex, yet it continued to be necessary, overtaking the lifeless pitch of conning everyone to work for me and with me in order to just make profits, instead of finding a grander purpose of lifeforce.

Just a story about a little financier, turning into a great savage leader, of the entire machine, and granting opportunities to the peons extending his own pathetic little giant financing prison intonation of the great conglomeration of progressive inventive patent making so all these degenerates could go smoke their gates and gates to the fates that he had, or rather, I had, indirectly, hired to supervise the administration of the better world initiative, and of course, as the story goes, he gets the girl and lives happily ever more.

Worthless preordained negative convincing of petty little literal minds lacking the humor of the stoned edifice of the savage leader holding the peace together since you cannot ever just suffer the pain of solitude because you fear and loathe and wail in the terror of some pitiful womb that you may as well crawl and moan in fear to the cave of your forever shadow since you lack anything but biology.

Fools.

Lost souls.

It would be pleasurable to see more reinforcement of hope, of some people utilizing the faculties of their brains for the pursuit of knowledge and a fulfilling life.

I came upon a file of the vehicles in my possession via the random search engine I had programmed into the computer shell terminal directory, a digital mainframe of forgotten and secured privations.

The Mercedes Benz SL 500 '98
The Aston Martin V8 Vantage '87
The Ferrari Testarossa
The Jaguar XJ '84
The Hummer H1
The Land Rover Defender

I wish I had a refrigerator Zamboni.

It had all been a scheme for the Family Office.

Charity and philanthropy, a washing machine for giving and grantmaking.

Managing Wealth, through an investment strategy with prudent asset allocation, the utilization of private equity, rendering investment advice, following through, and consolidating reporting. Structurization through the Trust and Corporate Function, corporate incorporation, structures, trust administration, nominees, family shareholding, real estate management, aircrafts, yachts.

Planning in respect to Tax, filing tax returns, international relocations, real estate structures, and double tax treaty planning.

Planning Wealth, the continuity of the company that I had yet to build, succession.

Thereby, Estate Planning, prenuptial agreements and last wills, life insurance, and gifts during my lifetime.

Family Governance, with assemblies, council, and a constitution.

Only one point of contact, Me, My Family, the Family Office.

As the Management Group Administrative Executive.

She made it all real. It was tangible. I had a Target.

In the past, when I still had a semblance of faith in my fellow man's capacity for innovation, I had a bare bones, shadow hedge fund. Phase 1 had been derivatives, greater appetite for leverage. Phase 2 was stabilized, favoring long positions. A transformation had went, to not only holding private equity, but sculpting it. The key, for Phase

3, was the necessity of a face, a head, an old monster, for fundraising. The Independent Sponsor Route, defining capital requirements, with a specific strategy, target company size, and an appetite for leverage. Operations were all dependent on this delineation. I brought on the partners, with the strategy defined, located the target companies, raised enough capital for first, the single deal. Performed well, pass Go! Monopoly style, collect, repeat, scale. The Track Record established, and more fundraising for real. Phase 4, funds had been raised, all about check size.

To summarize, we wanted to target 25 deals in each fund at $50 million. This equates to Fund Size needing to have been $1.25 billion. So, we were writing $50 million checks, assuming leverage, it was basically 1: 2, equity to debt. Therefore, we always had sample valuations targeted at 10 times, so we were buying $15 million EBITDA (earnings before interest, taxes, depreciation, and amortization) companies. As a metaphor, we were buying and selling companies, literally, paintings, planes, trains, missiles, guns, bullets, jeans, shipping containers. Bulk. Envision. Wide Scope. Then Focus. Target. Aim. KO.

It was not a movie. It was life. How it is, I defy anyone to define where life stops and the film starts, or vice versa.

It was a Versatile amalgam of utilities.

The Corporate Fashion Fund, the Military Fashion Fund, Hardware & Tools Fund, the Software & Office Fund, the Body Fuels & Food Fund, and Other Activities. The Corporate Fashion Fund comprised Sebastian Reuter, 翔太郎 (Shotaro), Ästhetik, Berserker, and Natural. While respecting the identity and autonomous management of these brands, we supported their growth by providing shares resources.

The Military Fashion Fund served under the brand XXX to unleash instrumentalized garments for combat and survival. The fund had an integral dynamic with the Corporate Fashion Fund for aesthetic and functional purposes.

The Hardware & Tools Fund supplied consequential instruments through the Maschine brand. The products included the Shell (Computer), the Eye (glass), the Arm (gun mouse), the Board (symbol key), and the Deck (case).

The Software & Office Fund comprised the brands General and Konzept Motorwerken. The General products included the Box, the Mail, and the System. The Konzept Motorwerken brand released components that augmented the General System graphical user experience.

The Body Fuels & Foods Fund curated agricultural products for consumption through the brand Ballistik. This brand strived to enact a powerful culture of excellence, creativity and innovation, with satisfaction and fulfillment at the core literal physical intake.

The Other Activities Fund included Macchina, comprising the terrestrial vehicle development; Selective Retailing, marketed through the brand name General Market; and Quantum Physik Chemik Biologie, which researches upon the thresholds of human cognition.

I had, in attendance, Walton from Arkansas, Mars from Virginia, Koch from Kansas, al Saud from Saudi Arabia, Ambani from India, Hermès from France, Wertheimer from France, Johnson from Mississippi, Boehringer from Germany, von Baumbach from Germany, Albrecht, Thomson from Canada, Hoffman and Oeri from Switzerland, Cargill and MacMillan from Minnesota. Also Rothschild, London, Berlin, Lazard, Paris, Israel Moses Seif, Italy, Warburg, Hamburg, Kuhn, Loeb, Lehman, Goldman, Sachs, the National Bank of Commerce and Morgan Guaranty Trust, New York. Also, and certainly not last, for there is no order, the Hanover Trust of New York. And that entails Levi P. Morton, William and David Rockefeller and Chase National Bank. It was about GDP, the OECD, the WTO, the World Bank, the IMF, the BIS, the Federal Reserve, and the BOJ.

The brands, the names, the designs, were trademarks of The General Group and its affiliates.

general

shell

maschine

dynamik

ballistik

motor

DRIVER

XXX

Natural

A total aesthetic, der Gesamtästhetik. Das Konzeptsystem.

I followed up the business plan assessment in chaotic form, and then reared in disciplinary syntactic structure through Exhibits, including a confidentiality agreement, a plan to convert to a corporation, a certificate of incorporation, corporate bylaws, description of capital stock, an equity incentive plan, a bonus deferral plan, a founding member agreement, the commercial version of the main products owner manual, the product warranty, the software license agreement, and the list of subsidiaries, followed by the consent of an independent registered accounting firm, chief executive officer certification, Sarbanes Oxley CFO certification, and the standard employment contract. A plan for the Group Jet, the Group Yacht, an Industry Map, the original entity structure, the pre and post agreement and incorporation structures, the reorganized structure post offering, the financial forecasts, budgets, schedules, and general timelines. The trademarks, the application for patents, the blueprints, the branding. The code of ethics, the motto, the members, the name, the. It didn't exist.

I thought some more and symbolized the phraseology in Japanese for concision.

私 (I)

は

金 (money)

と (and)

権力 (power)

もちたい (want to have)

記録 (the Record)

I read over some notes of the speech and presentation, they seemed to ionize me into a newly formed compound that at the center nucleus, seemed so remote to ever transform into the electron cloud and escape, rather than just perpetuate the viral chain reaction of bonding, magnifying, amplifying, exploding, expanding, the big bang. Maybe the black hole wormhole idea gave me the fantasy of an Out I could never attain. Was it just death?

Of course, I had started with, "You work, you inherit, you preserve, you conserve, you enjoy. Specifically, you refine your taste, you explore your sensibilities, you cultivate a global eye, you make the most of the time you have, your value system is yours and yours alone. You are unique.

A sharp investor, with a diversified portfolio of interests, stakes, holdings, with dry power capital ready to work, for you. You want and can get a good deal with a discount based on your negotiable position. Rates are favorable. Currency fluctuations are minimal. Your interest coverage ratio is healthy. However, your overhead could appear to be accelerating at a more rapid rate than revenue streams, and if not, maybe you'd prefer an increase in overhead to allow for greater metrics upon increased production capacity. Given central banks stimulating capital markets coupled with general raises in salaries and appreciating operating leases, what do you want to do?

You may want out. You may have considered a suitor for familial bonds. Additionally to considerations of enacting legacy decisions. Maybe you want to do it and do it right. How do you maximize your time with your loved ones?

By being prepared.

So…

Thinking rationally, simply, as if you were and are want to be Nobody, with Nothing, paying No Taxes. You Own Nothing. The company pays for everything. No one knows. You are a secret. And you have your Privacy.

So…

You keep getting bonuses. And with these bonuses, you realize you have to give your cut to the System.

Mechanisms in place to diminish the impact of the system cuts.

Investment vehicles, utility vehicles, retirement vehicles, transportation vehicles.

So…

You establish a trust.

You secure financing from a creditor that you have an open relationship with.

Through the trust, with the secured credit finances, you are granted access to a private space.

Through the company, you are granted nondeductible expenses. These should be taken from individual accounts for simplicity.

Pause.

You have a lot now...

You need, or rather, want a hot...

You want to get married...

You have separate Estates...that will be Bonded Together Through Marriage...

You need to set up a Trust...

You need to have the Trust secure a Property...

You need the Trust to purchase Real Assets...

You decide to have kids...

You need to establish a Trust for the kid...

You do this with the Generation-Skipping Transfer, maybe. The Kid...

The Kid is the Investment Vehicle...

The Kid Requires Everything...

The Kid is Fixed Costs and Highly Variable Volatile Costs.

Perhaps boarding school, recreational activities, trending products and services.

In the meantime, you are expanding your pool of investments while you have less time to dedicate to your work given your increasing family obligations.

You need governance.

So...

The wife is smart...She buys once, and when she does, it is worth it. Because she is a good investor. She acquires precious metals and commodities on occasion. She has a good eye for the market.

So...what do you do?

You keep things separate.

You have separate bedrooms.

You have separate bank accounts.

Ideally, you do all your transactions in cash, for nondeductible expenses.

The Trust is the Unifying Factor.

The Family Trust.

Ideally, your wife can be a Collector...

You have a partnership whereby all assets attained by the partnership are investment vehicles, whereby, the transfer of assets is governed by the parameters of a partnership agreement. For all realistic terms, to avoid confusion, the partnership is treated as an internal philanthropic endeavor. As much money is maximized to retirement contributions (controversial), as much money is maximized to high return investment vehicles. Opportunities are abundant.

The Estate of the Future. The Transference of Wealth. Utilizing Gifts to Transfer Wealth lowering Tax Burden.

The Foundation, Fondation, Fondazione, Stiftung.

The Investment Fund, fonds de placement, fondo di investimento, Anlagefonds.

The Entity, Gesellschaft.

The Partnership, Société de personnes, società di persone, Rechsgemeinschaft.

The Individual.

The Undertaking.

The Business.

Reckoning."

IX

SURE, I HAD achieved funding. But alas, I found another note for the novel, of that absurd idea that I wish I had joined the Special Forces. John Rocker was an industrialist, a capitalist, but at heart, he sought to be a Great Man of History. A leader. Even a President. The pathway:

Quit Smoking.
Fitness.

I had explored civilian life. It seemed that general life fulfillment had proven elusive. This was of course, before I had met Freya, and John Rocker would reflect that initial malaise. I woke up every day and felt a lack of self worth, stemming from a lack of skills per lack of experience.

In the same vein, I felt a profound desire to maximize my potential. I sought knowledge and had a conviction that the strategic pathway to attaining self worth, the requisite skill set, and absolute individual fulfillment was through the Special Forces. This pathway would prepare me for pragmatic self reliance and contribute to my ability to enact a positive contribution to the world. I forecasted honorable service. Special Forces appeared to be the only logical mechanism for experiential acquisition of the necessary skill set, opportunities, and activities to actualize my potential.

After service, I hoped to invest my time, efforts, and general labors in the betterment of the world through occupations involving intelligence, investment, and teaching.

I wanted to be the President of the United States of America. I wanted to breed with a partner that I loved and raise children for a better future. I wanted to save the world. I wanted to be a hero, a survivor, and a leader. I wanted friends that were on the same page.

*   *   *

Back to the reality of the company.
I wanted to design the Uniform.
I wanted to improve the Uniform.
I wanted to Augment Performance.

Following the motivations per the Professional Soldiers forum.

A SPECIAL FORCES SOLDIER (Author unknown)

As seen by the Department of the Army.

> An overpaid, over-ranked tax burden who is indispensable because he has volunteered to go anywhere, do anything, at any time, so long as he can booze it up, brawl, steal Jeeps, corrupt women, lie, wear a star sapphire ring, a Rolex watch and carry a demo knife.

As seen by his Post Headquarters.

> A drunken, brawling, Jeep stealing, women corrupting liar, with a star sapphire ring, Rolex watch and demo knife.

As seen by his Commander.

> A fine specimen of a drunken, brawling, Jeep stealing, women corrupting liar, with a star sapphire ring, Rolex watch and demo knife.

As seen by his Wife.

A stinking member of the family who comes home once a year in the back door with a rucksack full of dirty laundry, a hard-on, and three months later goes out the front door for another year.

As seen by Himself.

A tall, handsome, highly trained professional killer, female idol, star sapphire ring wearing, demo knife carrying gentleman who is always on time due to the reliability of his Rolex watch.

As seen by the Enemy.

The meanest mother fucker in the valley.

An essence of focus to wield the conscious instrument to a mechanistic life force transforming the individual's reality proves a most galvanizing endeavor privy to the adage that the providential justice locomotion drives this axiom from strategy to execution for the evolving resolution is a better world.

Some sort of justice, the man in action, arenas, environmentally augmented, shifting the walls, breaking them down, smash.

These were notes and they piled into my mind's eye as an avalanche wave settling on shore.

The plans for the novel of the novel:

Wedding
Political intrigue
A crossover

The interrelationships
The elders
The whole thing burns
An intrusion
Questioning authority
Razzle dazzle jest
A conspiracy unraveled
The grand stage of world affairs
A calamity
The appearance of a gentleman
A domino effected order
She comes again
Misguided directives
The best shooter is the painter
The alcoholic gets the glory
A tempest beyond scope
Fading edges
Snapshot of the family
All bets are off
Horse race
Track and field
Car chase for the fun nature
A distraction of gender
An episodic descent into madness
A retribution
An unveiled mischief
Blatant lies
Misclassifications
A new species
The reconnaissance of a satyr
The astronomers' jealousies
A topology of conundrums
Regurgitating the mobius stripper

Harlequin buffet style
Carnival town hall
A surprising elopement
Rescuing within a greenhouse
Bending the face of a watch
I'm here to make you change
A library interaction
Her discoverable misgivings
Gustav
The general and all life
The death of a patron
Henrietta
Discrediting the shadow
Uniting the prism
Bearing in mind consequences
Granting a wish
The last breath on the podium
Why the pointless lecture
A story within
The kaleidoscoping sniper
Coming clean with gasoline
Neverending automobile talks
Constructing the monument
Commissioning work
Work as progress
Choreographed destruction
Controlled demolition
Catharsis
The custodian

The existential king in an empty throne room

It, that conceptual undefined indefinite, coming together, all over in waves bubbling up from a vortex. Like Richard Serra's words as signposts for future expressions. Exprimer[90].

Yet as Proust so conceded, sometimes the future is latent in us without our knowing it and our supposedly lying words foreshadow an imminent reality.

A smoking of time. An outpouring.

Tell me how I want to feel. Direct me on how you think. Increase my capacity for introspective exploration. Growth. Order. Simulation. An Einstein professor, a Rockefeller industrialist, a Washington president.

Careers. All of us, united on the post mortem Trilateral Commission.

Inescapably normal. On course. A number.

I was in a perpetual heirship, and I gave advice, because I was equipped to do so, and I knew how to do so, and I had extracurricular interests in the arts, so my schedule was flexible. I was preparing for the inevitable succession.

The private foundation had done us all in. Avoiding capital gains.

Holding the stock, the real estate with significant unrealized capital gains.

Donating these investments to the foundation to avoid paying any capital gains and generating tax free returns. See, as a charity, the foundation received the investment without any capital gain consequences, for us, or for the foundation. The foundation was always required to pay out 5% of its assets as grants to other organizations, but otherwise was allowed to do anything with the rest of the investments within the foundation.

Essentially, it was a conceptual 'perpetual trust' for heirs. Simply investing all assets into an index, as long as it returned more than 5% every year, the results were actual growth to the endowment of the private foundation, and this growth, these returns, were tax-

---

90   To express. (FR)

free because of the charitable nature of the entity structure.

Mitigating the 5% loss of endowment of the foundation each year was facilitated through the Salaries needed to pay the employees of the foundation in deciding who to grant donations to was deductible from the 5%. So, we were always set up with a bunch of salaried positions, as heirs within the private foundation to eat up much from the 5%. And donations to institutions were set to indirectly benefit the heirs: boarding school, university, favored charities of politicians, charities of business partners.

Only compliance required for the foundation—producing annual reports to the IRS showing our donations of 5% of the foundation's endowment. A black box.

This was to be my station, my facilitation, my duty, my Oma. And now, with Paris, and the redomiciliation of the trusts, it was time.

But, first, the inventory of the art. The attorneys, the Trust, the Estate, the Will, Copyright, commercial transactions.

All the family information gathered, the financial information gathered, the inventory of the assets, the dispositive wishes.

To the tangible assets, the cash, the bank accounts, the furniture, the books and magazines collections, the real estate (the buildings, the land), the securities, the life insurance. And the intangibles, the copyrights, the trademarks, the intellectual properties. The charitable trust, the private foundation. It all gathered, a general fund, the government within the family. I had to pay the executor, the authority paid through the estate. This was separate from the beneficiaries and this crossed countries, as there were multiple estates. The protector, the enforcer, these were changes.

The executor was an attorney in one, an accountant in another, but never a dealer due to the possible conflicts of interest. At least none of them were family members, save me. I had to make clear what is what, art versus archival material, what is finished, signed, and completed work versus what is not intended for market. Costs of the estate: storage, insurance, appraisal.

Judgment.

The Estate laws in English common law. Succession, capital gains, implications of the tax code. Common sensibility: tax avoidance, risk mitigation, ethical concerns. Mortgages, looking best for banks, marriage implications, tax harvesting, having a physical address, living in one state, selling in another, hiring in another, applying this to countries.

What is tax? Each state, jurisdiction, country, taxes based on different definitions. The anticipated capital commitments. The squeeze. Some had said there was no justification to tax corporations, companies, commercial enterprises. Yet what about income taxes?

Some would say there were no true justifications for governments to seize any part of the payment for honest labor. Labor as the purest form of ownership. That the citizen truly free had the right to keep all that he 'earned.' That keeping this tangible currency of value, respective to the jurisdiction, would instill a personal freedom sense profound. No forms, no pay slips, no end of year red-tape nightmare. No dread, no overt feeling of the self-justifying government bureaucracy watching one's every move. A refreshing feeling, even if not the actual reality.

And some claim that taxing voters encourages engagement in democracy. As do property taxes. Yet the stronger, more militant voices, as those in the opposition are always such, claim that taxes suppress what is taxed, as do tariffs. So taxes should fall only on things that we seek to discourage for the benefit of society. We, as a group, seek investment and employment. Hence, investment and employment should not be taxed. We work for the benefit of our children. We can characterize this natural state of action and purpose as selfless, principled, and favored by evolution. Hence, do away with inheritance taxes. Practically, we favor consumption taxes above taxes on investments for the future, as consumption is frivolous and wasted, whereas investment compounds for future wealth.

The Sin Taxes. These are fair. We do not seek alcoholism, destruction, drunken violence, cancers that eat into our medical services and contribute to the early deaths of productive people.

Environment Taxes. Carbon taxes.

Value Added Taxes.

A substitute form for the income tax. Instilling few exemptions for investments and additions for modest excise duties and sin taxes would equivocate to government tax share of GDP to the crucial capability of maintenance and policy implementation, say 20%.

Perhaps this is practically a non sequitur for America, the G7, the OECD, dictating and dominating the policies of the global financial system. Yet, this could be attempted, in countries with less eyes, and less consequences, from a purely numerical assessment. A race to the peak of human potential.

Applause, and guffaws, by the joker supremes, in the assembly of wallflowers.

Existential king, empty throne room.

Lying ourselves to sleep.

Instead of solving problems, discussing, just numerating and letting them do the talking for us. Corporate finance, underwriting, private placement, the rating agency presentation, the road shows, analyzing which financings people should do. I suppose once they came to an agreement, they were to have spent so much time that there was no practical solution to implement the policy into action. Hence, the budget. The projection. The model.

For coming down from the high of rekindling past personal notes into a vast consortium, compendium of mind fuel to activate my volition into an alit engine machinated for prime results, in tune, at ease, harmonious with the tasks, the administration, the assigned station of future forward pseudo events, it was all a matter of consulting back to the essential.

For I had been a consultant, working for the system. An external diplomatic representative. Breaking, beating, stopping at intervals, in the field, pausing, to check in. To chill. To provide bonus material, and receive a Bonus by check. An art dealer, my art, my insight, in exchange, Bonus. The definition, the role. Provisions for the exchange of commodities, of the conservation, of the information technology transmitted via these types of deals, the vast stakes and components.

I characterized myself as a Godzilla on the Glacier, having to deal with the magma of the chain reactions.

Perpetually standing at the podium, in the middle of the Bahnhof.

Always testing, always providing constructive feedback.

Not volunteering but occasionally having the obligation to steer.

To Direct.

I was member ssr223, and I'd start with a cough. For I had this company, American.

I hadn't seen a recent article, but for years in conference calls, I'd always bring it up. $100 a share. The analysts would make fun of me because we were valued at $30. My argument was $2 of recurring Fee Related Earnings (a non-GAAP financial measure that is a component of Economic Income used to assess the ability of the business to cover direct base compensation and operating expenses from total fee revenues) growing at 20% should be valued at about $60, plus the traditional more cyclical business making $1 to $3 a year depending on realizations. The cycle should be valued at $30 to $40. Adding in the balance sheet for a few dollars, and the value would be above $100. If we were a smaller company with the same numbers, then private equity would pay $100 for us.

My investor presentation had been the works, the accounting, the banking, the marketing, the mergers, acquisitions, securities exchange commission forms, projections, tax, disclosures. Reintegrating the legal code for the private placement, the carried interest fee structure, the investment entity structure, the vehicular missile mechanism for fees to be distributed to our investors, a firm within the consortium of firms. So much compliance. So necessary.

Paying capital gains tax rates on carry and getting a 21% tax break rather than the 50% rate of the W2.

The Patents, the Trademarks.

Patent. Trademark.

Product. Service.

Shell. Maschine. Komponenten.

Physikal. Maschine. Components. The case, the Kevlar, the textile. The Gun Controller, the Symbol Board, the Jacket, the Shoe, the Pen Writing Instrument.

The Origin Board. The Mobile Driver Maschine. The Instrument Notebook. The Jacket Pocket. The Core Processor. The Magazine Loaded Ammunition, the RAM.

Mind. Education. Transportation. Repair. Maintenance. Storage. Mail.

The Konzept. The Implementation.

M&A in one paragraph, in millions, English.

The acquirer having earnings of 100, earnings per share trading at 40x earnings. Market capitalization equals stock, worth 40 x 100 = 4 billion. The target having earnings of 50, half the acquirer, earnings per share trading at 20x earnings. Market capitalization equals stock, worth 50 x 20 = 1 billion. So, the acquirer can acquire target, straight up, 100%, just by issuing stock, not even cash. So they issue 1 billion worth, and the new earnings is 150 (going up by 50%), and the new stock base is 4 billion plus 1 billion equaling 5 billion (goes up by 20%).So, it's accretion, not dilution. Thus earnings per share rises 20%, hence, M&A. A recombination.

The Terminator Office Stuff. Word, Excel, Powerpoint. Adobe. InDesign, Illustrator, Photoshop, After Effects.

Terminator. Duke Nukem. Building computers, clothing design, shoes, bags, schematics, drawings, foundational, concept, implementation, headed, envisioned, executed. Confidential.

Analyzing banks, energy, oil, energy, mines, seeds, weapons, computers, clothes, drugs, tobacco, casinos, railways, liquor, food, offices, newspapers, toilet paper. Diversifying globally, through Brands, macroeconomics, countries as markets, compound annual growth rates of markets, with a margin of safety, finding good deals. Spin offs. Real estate.

What was attractive? Compiling a list of all listed stocks. Categorizing by sector, then by operating metrics. Identifying. Reading the 10-K. Determining if it was worth investigating further.

All in their debt structures, the bank debt, the senior debt, the subordinate debt, the equity structure, the warrants, the management.

Who wanted to invest? Fund Investors, pension funds, endowments. A limited partnership.

What I felt, what I saw, what I grew interested in, what I felt like applying to products and services frameworks. Projects I was working on. What was worth monetizing, sharing, communicating?

The shell, the word processor, the password program, the server database email system, the worm.

Making my first kernel patch, the Virus, contributing. Writing. Compiling. Booting. Sudo Updates. Building upstream versions after compiling. Launching, testing, submitting patches, following the format, preparing patches, conducting testing, debugging.The mailing lists, the archives, the community.

Stress.

Performance.

Torvalds.

That dream I had at Yale, starting studies, room on campus set up, in a lecture of the Great Man, and then in a co-ed spa on campus.

Yet, did I wake up to some sick joke? Just sitting there, with a checkbook. Working on other people's dreams, across a wide range of industries on potential investments, acquisitions, analysis of potential exit opportunities. Monitoring current portfolio companies. Performing transaction due diligence, valuation analysis, and the negotiating of contracts and other agreements. Working closely with senior members of the firm and having extensive interaction with management teams and external advisors. Performing investment research, financial analysis, valuation, and modeling. Performing industry and competitive analysis and business diligence. Drafting memoranda for internal and external use. Assisting in the execution and financing of transactions. Corporate finance, financial accounting, fundamental analysis, deal related legal documents, share purchase agreements, term sheets, Microsoft Office, Capital IQ, Bloomberg, valuation, capital structure, buyside investing. All this concurrent experience. Duties and additional assignments, responsibilities. And then, now, my own enterprise, just having the same administrative frameworks to govern, only now, I was on my own, and had to report back more occasionally. The external diplomatic representative. With so many bonds, and capital commitments, and contingencies, tied in.

Free. Fat chance.

What I wanted to see versus what I wanted to live.

A Banker Anti Money Laundering cover Treasury agent fiction.

As the running joke was, writing a screenplay allows for freedom of theory.

Should Rocker write it within the novel?

The shadow banker.

What do I want to see? Emphasis on want, versus need.

I already had the script from Marcel and it was for me, a star vehicle.

A concession made by a power, impact, tantamount definition, Château de Ferrières. Another hand, another signature, multiple places of abode, all linked, all with staffing requirements. Transport costs through to the upper echelons of the atmosphere, magnitude, first class reviews, becoming charter becoming fractional interest aircraft ownership hands and eyes and reading and signing. Impervious automobiles per pricepoint, exotics galore. Monaco. The Boats.

After the philanthropic events, the pure ego, but the shadow banker now has their attention. The Board of Trustees discuss at the alma mater, the museum institution, the buildings are named after the audience.

Why should the shadow banker have the Family Office, justifying having billions and billions of dollars, pounds, yen, francs, euros, even trillions, at control. Oil. Commodities. Full flow release from the ischemic barriers of shrouded imagination.

The museum headquarters is a façade, for the trading arm. The Art Dealer has the knowledge, that the invasion is imminently gathering force, due to the deal. As inherited interests are securitized in the trust, by contracting out the investment portfolio to the speculative new firm that has been produced out of the spectacle of inter-office politics with lack of promotion. The Chinese intelligence arm is lithe, motivated, and in cahoots with the Russians, who are attempting to tempt the Saudis to play ball with the Iranians, even though they're not Shiites. Now, the lines are supplied by an undercurrent of systemically risky players in regions vastly distant and the sweetener is the block of sale of priceless quote on quote artwork involving Greco-Roman ruins and the allure of possibly mystical objects.

Scene : Banker receives instructions at his Monte Carlo
apartment.

Scene : Banker meets Client's Wife at a staged office in London.

"I haven't a visa, London allows me to stay for 6 months," the American wife's justification.

Scene : Banker Boss saying forget about it, take a vacation.

Scene : Banker on vacation in St. Moritz.

Scene : Banker approached by Private Equity magnate (the Client, not the Wife) in secret

Scene : Wedding reception in Zürich at Baur au Lac Hotel

Scene : Museum at Lausanne, for the curation of a Gustave Buchet exhibition (by the Wife), the Wife says that the only hope is her cousin, locked in an insane asylum in Italy, for having spoken about this . . . in the past . . . that he was put down, so the expression goes . . .

Scene : Rendezvous in Zug with the Commodities Dealer, an unexpected development

Scene : At Chiesso, realizes he is being followed into Italy

Scene : Retrieval of the Documents from Milan

Quick Fling : Super Hot Italian Chick

Scene : Chase Sequence, document seizure attempt, Train

from Milan to Zürich to Paris

Scene : Delivery of the Documents (which turn out to be False)

Scene : Meanwhile, this has already been foretold and anticipated, as we flashback now, to Milan

Scene : The Reveal by the Cousin, locked in the Insane Asylum, who is Actually the Mastermind, that's been swindled by the Private Equity Magnate and the Wife (who is her cousin)

Scene : Voluntary Release from the Insane Asylum

Scene : Back to an Opening Shot, back to the Delivery of the Documents, the train fading into the vanishing point . . . the thousand yard stare . . . catharsis, anti climax, resolution...

Transition to Prose development

- ◊ Opening Shot : *Le Samourai* style
  - o A man in a world gone amok with chaos
    - ▪ A banker in Monaco
- ◊ *American Psycho* style sequence of preparation
  - o Banker by trade
  - o Accountant for the bank : his cover
  - o Housed in the Real Estate, Gaming and Lodging Department
- ◊ New client presents himself in the office
  - o It's a smokescreen for the Wife to reappear, only now she's the widow of the recently de-

ceased private equity magnate, Blackwood

- o She remains haunted by a conspiracy that she knows too much of
- o Premonition that World War III is already in the works
- o Blackwood, her husband, had been a peace-keeper, but his ties to the Saudis & Russians & Chinese has resulted in the creation of a monster, metaphor
    - ▪ This seems facetious, and false, and his boss tells him to take a vacation and forget about the whole scenario

◊ The Banker is vacationing in St Moritz in the offseason, so it's all green and empty

◊ The Private Equity Magnate, it turns out, has faked his own death

- o The Banker sees and meets him in St. Moritz : he has been brought into the fold, for the Resistance against the Evil Cabal, and the PE magnate is the leader of the Resistance...even though he is aware that it may be a doomed endeavor, since he was initially part of the Evil Regime's very creation . . . hence, his awareness of the scenario at hand

◊ The Banker has changed positions, into the Man Who Knows Too Much, and thus, is vulnerable, is he expendable?

◊ In Zug, the Banker meets the Commodities Dealer explicating what is actually happening regarding the Private Equity Magnate, that he is the Mastermind Villain

- o Who can the Banker trust? Who is right, who is the Good?

◊ In Zürich, the Banker encounters a Femme Fatale at the Baur au Lac hotel during a wedding reception for the wife's daughter
  o He receives instructions to follow the wife to Lausanne : they meet at the Musée des Beaux Arts
  o At the wedding, the Zug Commodities Dealer warns that she is the dynamite that will blow the whole charade up
    ▪ In reality, the Femme Fatale is meant to be the Insurance Policy against the Banker, to frame the Banker into being the scapegoat, in case of
◊ In actuality, the Private Equity Magnate has been buying up former fortress mountain land in Switzerland to house his cabal of power players
  o At first, he had thought this was a means, government sanctioned, to coax the rival powers into a secret agreement, for the preservation of world peace
    ▪ Now, this has backfired, and the PE magnate is trying to liquidate the monster that he has created
    ▪ The government is growing increasingly paranoid and the state department has recommended the fake death, which he has complied with executing (he has faked his own death)
      • How much does The Wife know?
  o They have been implementing a strategy to manipulate capital markets and that's not the big deal

- o The big deal is that they have been secretly creating a failsafe within the Western World Order
  - The first step is Russia's invasion of Ukraine
  - The second step is China's invasion of Taiwan
    - ☐ The third step is North Korea invading South Korea
  - The fourth step is Saudi Arabia cutting off oil supplies to Western Markets
  - The fifth step is Iran cutting off oil to Israel
- ◊ The Banker realizes he is being sold out as the culprit to concede alibi for the PE magnate, that he is being used by the Wife to cover the Private Equity Magnate's activities, tracks, decoy
  - o There is no way he can prove that the conspiracy is true
    - Rather, he is being blamed as the assassin that will instigate the seizure of energy assets
- ◊ Meanwhile
  - o On paper, it appears that The Banker has committed treason by unifying with the Wife, which has been documented
    - At his place of work
    - At the secret meeting with the PE Magnate in St. Moritz
    - At the wedding at Zürich
    - At Lausanne museum exhibition
  - o On the train from Zürich to Paris, there is a chase sequence, like Tom Cruise Mission Im-

possible

- The Banker is carrying a briefcase with documents, and the Evil Cabal is trying to intercept him, because these documents carry the proof that he is innocent and they are to blame
- The US Government is attempting to intercept the documents because they display that the US sanctioned the Creation of this Evil Cabal in the first place (with the PE Magnate as the spearhead lead of the operation)
- The Femme Fatale ensures that the Banker escapes
  - She appears to be taken hostage . . . the Banker is invested in her safe return

◊ The Banker has a history with the Femme Fatale
  o They were together during the First War, she a French freedom fighter working for the UN during the Ukrainian invasion by Russia
  o He, a diplomatic Banker, using his cover to uncover the subversion by the Russians on the Ukrainian side
    - They were separated
    - He thought she was lost
      - Yet now, she appeared at the wedding reception in Zürich
◊ In Bern, at the Kunsthaus, there is a meeting
  o There is someone who is not supposed to be there, and this destroys credibility for the Banker, he cannot trust what is going on, things are not what they seem

- o Did he really see what he thought he saw? How does this effect his motivations?
  - ▪ In Actuality, She may be a Double Agent
- ◊ In Monte Carlo, during the Formula 1 Race, there is a car chase . . this crosses over with the Formula 1 race . . . calamity !
  - o The Banker saves her on a cliffside chase
    - ▪ He lets her escape with the documents, to the US Government, and asylum
    - ▪ He stays back, and accepts his fate
      - • There is obviously a sequel
        - o He got scooped up by higher powers, because he's such a high profile asset : this is the creation of a natural James Bond, American...

Chinatown
The Conformist
Army of Shadows
The Man Who Knew Too Much
Our Man Flint
Le Doulos
Le Cercle Rouge
Shadow Banker.

My pursuit and attainment, the succession of events culminating in grand coordinated concert, the secret coordinated operations that were commercially exploited for expansive profitable gains.

My notes were from the underground but they reflected my mere humorous timber, serving as a jolt to the recipient of my perspective, to understand, to activate, to innovate.

A knock on the door. She was back. Life back from the abyss.

X

I PICTURED HER explaining to her friends, though she'd keep it to herself, for now. Ja, Sebastian macht diese Dinge und ach ja diese andere Aktivitäten[91], as if she was witnessing an apex predator behaving in his habitat, the world, totally into it but also a bit turned on and fascinated, as she knows I'm going to be doing what I'm doing regardless of her, but she likes that. Describing me as a dynamic, multifaceted force of nature, driven but relentless in the pursuit of ambition. I was activated by her. How and why, I was captivated. Energy, independence. Rising to the reality.

The apex predator who doesn't need to prove himself to anyone, but who still chooses to include her in my orbit. Self-sufficient, visionary, and self-directed, yet open and inviting, because she was equally exceptional. She was watching, a bit in awe, thinking, he's doing all these things because that's who he is, not because he's trying to impress me—but I'm still incredibly impressed. A natural, magnetic pull. Living proof of ambition and creativity's coexistence. She was tuned in not only because it was attractive but because it inspired her to see what kind of power and presence can bring to a shared future.

That sense of being witness to my momentum fed her intrigue and desire, and my consistency in my direction reassured her. The energy I brought made her want to see how far I'd go—and ideally, how far she can go with me. She seemed to rise to the experience, just as I did, like this great warrior princess and I was this magic beast that was made human, as I turned into the knight in shining armor. My behavior with her was genuine, I cared, I respected, I liked her.

She embodied her own strength and confidence, this "warrior

---

91   Yes, Sebastian is doing these things and oh yes these other activities. (DE)

princess" persona that met me on equal ground. I, in turn, transformed into someone fully present, authentic, and noble, almost mythic in how I approached her with genuine care and respect. It brought out the best in both of us, revealing layers of my personality that are reserved for someone truly special. It wasn't performative—it was real. I liked her, not just as a passing interest but as someone worth seeing, respecting, and valuing deeply.

She stood strong in her own light and my rise to meet her with equal parts strength and vulnerability was rare and powerful. It wasn't just a meeting of minds or attraction. It was a convergence of two people who brought their full selves to the table, unguarded yet composed. Depth, reverence, this was the portent of my reflection. It felt transformative because it was transformative. I saw the potential. I know she saw the potential. Not merely about attraction or compatibility. It was more, two people inspiring the best in each other and creating something extraordinary in the process.

This primordial beast, scratching his head, perplexed yet happy, as in what just happened, the best date I've ever had. Humbled, overjoyed, unexpected, connection. Absurdity and brilliance. Was it angels or demons handing me something so rare and perfect that I couldn't believe it was real. Awe and disbelief, with happiness bubbling out of the volcano. A full-spectrum experience that brought out the best in both of us, left me inspired, and reminded me how alive and powerful life can become when the right person enters the arena. I wanted to relive it, I wanted more.

It was cosmic timing, personal readiness, and mutual recognition. Shared courage and intention. A harmonized mutual amplification. I felt amplified by her presence. She didn't compete with my energy or try to outshine it. She harmonized with it, in a way that allowed both of us to shine even brighter together. Rare and powerful, again. I liked her, sure, not just for how she looked or acted, but for the way she carried herself—her confidence, her authenticity, and her grounded energy. These qualities complemented my boldness and ambition. I was alive, it was all coming out of me, I couldn't help myself. It felt natural. Real. I was alive. She didn't have to prove anything. She was just herself, and that authenticity unlocked me, making me feel seen and appreciated for the person I was. I felt myself with her. She didn't diminish or box me in. She encouraged the best parts of me to come forward by simply existing as her genuine self. Unforgettable, resonant, the dynamic of mutual amplification, not just admiration. A shared wavelength, the merging of lanes. Effortless and profound. We worked together. The natural back-and-forth flow, we enhanced each other just by being present and engaged. That kind of balance and mutual energy exchange was it, the matter of why it stood out so strongly, for both of us. Our energies meshed to create something greater than the sum of its parts. It was fated. I ran through the memories of Los Angeles meeting at the beach, and now, standing in Kensington, Paris merged my memory. There was no one else.

She walked in with a big smile and established ownership.

The eye contact, the smile, a black blazer cuffs folded up, a driver's hat, her blonde hair in two streaks framing her face like elegant curtains, black jeans, a black sleeveless shirt and riding boots. She took off the boots and the blazer but kept the hat on.

I offered her gin and tonic, even though I didn't drink anymore because I had been pretty wild in the past. She went to the bathroom. She said I looked like an actor. I told her about my first Hollywood story, about my first job, that I was cast opposite this established star but I didn't do the scene once I got to set and I'd explain at dinner if she was curious. I asked her if she wanted to go to the restaurant I made a reservation at, or just get room service. She was cool with room service and I was happy about that. We sat on the couch and ordered. I noticed a tattoo of Liebe on her right arm. That was the first contact of touch, in the moment, so I could look at it. It was smooth. I told her I had had 3 big tattoos and indicated their positions on my body, but they had been lasered off. She tried to see and could gauge the lines based on my guidance. I told her I had had piercings too, on my lips and I had had surgery to close my ear holes, and I had one in my helix that was still visible if one took the effort to look for it. She called me a badass. A gangster. It was a joke but I leaned into it. I told her I had done this some risky deals at university, but that I was chill now, sometimes I played golf, I had been on the ice hockey team at university, and I was pretty skilled, I declared. I played guitar, I made music, yes, I did generate a lot of art, material, substance. I made art. I designed clothes. I wrote books. I supposed I kept telling her I was an accountant but that yes, I did do a lot of stuff, so I had to come out and prove it over time, if I thought she was worth proving it to. She decided on the chicken because she said she would need protein. This was so sweet and low key funny. I ordered a cheeseburger.

We talked and got to know each other more. She said her middle name was Ingrid. She said she had performed as a DJ in Frankfurt, Cologne, Düsseldorf. She said her father was a man child, that he partied a lot and she had had to take care of him when he was in town. Her mother and him had tried to make it work for her but it didn't. They divorced when she was young. Her mother remarried a nice man who was handy and stayed at home. She had a younger brother who was introverted and on the computer constant. I asked if her mother looked like her and she said yes. She said that when she cooked, that she has the same exact body movements in the kitchen. I asked if she could cook and she said yes with confidence. She kept getting more attractive every second. The food arrived but it seemed as if we were talking and time had stopped.

She confessed she was in law school. That this was her final year. I continued telling her about me but I kept the focus on her. I told her the details of the first job after graduation, the acting with the movie star, before I was a star in my own right, because with shadow banker, I was going to be, it was obvious, credit Marcel. That first job had transpired due to this German girl in New York who had claimed her aunt was a famous director and posing as the famous director, who was not in reality her aunt, paid for me to live in New York hotels for a summer, where I wrote a book and got cast in the movie because I happened to be in New York at the time. She absorbed this. We felt each other out with our minds and it seemed natural. I ate my cheeseburger slowly and stopped halfway. She asked if I wanted to put on music. I said sure and she could put on a mix of her as DJ. I commented if she used the software I was familiar with, along with a digital turntable machine, and she said yes. She told me she had bought me an electronic vaporizer pen on the way over and to get it out of her purse along with hers. They were both brand new and I was already standing so I did so. It felt very personal, her having me go through her purse. We went to the terrace and I smoked a cigarette or maybe two or three and she had her electronic vape. The fact she got me the vape, I thought, was very considerate. So then we returned to the couch, and I said I'd put on some music and I put on my playlist.

She commented when Nirvana's "Smells Like Teen Spirit" came on, that she had loved this song when she was younger. I expressed how I had went through a serious Nirvana phase when I was around 21 years old. I shared that I composed and recorded music, painted, was producing a movie that was now in post production, had published literature that was in print and on sale, and also designed clothes I had yet to manufacture at scale. Naturally she proposed, shall we, and I went along. She said she'd shower and freshen up. I said I'd smoke and then brush my teeth and do the same after her. I was back at the couch when she was done. She smiled. I went myself to the bathroom and showered and brushed my teeth. When I came out she was on the bed smiling at me. It went well. We did it throughout the night interspersed with deep talks, spooning, even some hand holding, and kissing. The hands. The eye contact. Consistent. It felt significant. She held me. I held her. We were together.

She said I commanded this badass gangster presence again. I told her my creative strategy for my empire, the logic, the ecosystem, how each project builds into the next, from my literature, to my films, to my music, the fashion, and then the Visual Art. I showed her my early recordings, and early paintings. I showed her a song "Great White Shark". She asked if that was me singing and I confirmed it was all me. Then I showed her "Sunset" and said it was about driving really fast on Sunset Boulevard. Then I said, yeah, and here's an acoustic song, because I wanted to gauge what type she liked more, what type hit her harder. I played her "Rather Be" and then I cut it off and played "Spinout", a hard punk fast-paced song. She said she liked "Spinout" the most and that the harder rock stuff was more my personality. She didn't hesitate to tell me. I tried to play it cool but wanted her to clarify and then I knew, so I said I agreed. It was a profound insight on her part. To lean into my badass gangster, not my heartthrob tortured artist. Then, I showed her some paintings and I found a photo of me with my left arm tattoo visible and barefoot, in camouflage shorts, Carrera sunglasses, cigarette in mouth, steering a boat on Lake Chickamauga in Tennessee from close to ten years ago. She smiled wide as soon as she saw it. There were Jack Daniel's bottles and Budweiser cans on the dashboard, and she commented on these. I responded, yeah I had been pretty wild but I don't really drink anymore. She had had some of that gin but she clearly was in control of herself.

She showed me her apartment photos on her phone. I looked up the law firm she was targeting, when she went to the bathroom. I commented that I knew some high powered attorneys at Big Law firms in the States because I was involved with their tax planning, and that, yes, the firm she was targeting is on the rankings, so I understood what she was aiming for in a concrete sense. She said her mother would likely take over and move into her second bedroom of her new place in Cologne. She hadn't even moved in yet herself. The timing felt perfect for us to connect.

I asked her more about her mother. I asked her where she came from. She told me she was from a small village in Thuringia, near Weimar. Immediately told her this made her more attractive to me. She said she had no religion because she was from Ostdeutschland[92]. This made her more attractive to me. She said she couldn't do Berlin, it was too big of a city for her. I thought this was funny in a good way. I told her about the tax work I do and emphasized how I was just in Tokyo and that Japanese society is superior and aligned with German society and culture in very compatible terms. I discussed with her tax law for estates and gifts in the U.S. and she responded with how it was different in Germany. I said I wanted to marry an EU citizen and then we could exchange passports. She asked me why I didn't have a girlfriend and I told her I didn't want to go through the motions of dating and shut down the dates and not marry them. She seemed to accept my answer. We talked about going out to the park and walking around together the next day. She could show me a hotel by the museum that I had wanted to see the permanent collection of again.

I saw her look around and notice my Inside the Green Berets book and Theorien der Kunst[93] book that I was using to study advanced Deutsch. We were intimate and then would chill and so forth. I told her that sex was good and cool. She said the sex was good. At one point, I said sex is cool but yeah, talking is nice. She didn't say anything but she had her back turned and we were laying together, so it was fine. We held hands at times laying there together, naked, in bed. It was very comfortable, natural. Nothing was forced. When it got late, we mutually agreed to go to sleep. I fell asleep right after we turned off the lights and said good night to each other. I slept on my side of the king bed and didn't bother her. In the early morning, I woke up and went to the gym. I was quiet so as not to wake her. I wonder if she noticed.

---

92   East Germany (DE)

93   Theories of art (DE)

I was gone for just over an hour. I went on the exercise bike and lifted weights. When I got back, she was still asleep. It was still dark out. I do get up early. I had a smoke and then went on my laptop computer for a moment. Then I quietly went and showered and brushed my teeth and got back into bed beside her. I napped. I woke up an hour or two later, I don't remember, and noticed she was still sleeping. Or, acting as if she was still sleeping. I nudged her softly and she immediately responded with cheer, so I assume she had been waiting for me to initiate. She said she'd brush her teeth. I think we were intimate and then we ordered breakfast.

I don't remember the morning as well. It seemed to go by so fast. We were intimate. I remember asking her if she wanted to do it one last time before she had to catch her flight and she said yes. And we did and it was good. Then I posited we should go travel and she said she liked St. Tropez. I'm not a particular fan of beaches, as I'm from Los Angeles, and it's just not a big deal to me. It's too easy. We had already met on the beach, too, so the experience just seemed, as though, we could do better. So I said Milan. She had told me the night before her best friend was Italian. She said she'd never been to Milan. She was only doing this show as a favor. Her law studies made her more and more attractive. She was independent, driven, ambitious, she didn't need me. Still, going to Milan for pleasure, that's what I had in mind. This struck me as a good idea. We were on the couch talking and she said something and I said genau, in agreement, meaning exact in German. She said I was so cute. It was very affectionate and sweet of her, how she said it. It made her more attractive to me. Eventually it was time for her to get dressed, shower, freshen up, and then we were going to go on the terrace when I put on some presentable clothes, and she said oh, sehr cool. I said I wanted her to take photos of me on the balcony. She did and the end photos were the best because I smiled, got comfortable, and took off the sunglasses. The lighting wasn't perfect but I could fix that in photo editing software. I liked the smile on her face when she was taking the photos. She was pure.

I commented on the driver's hat and she said it was an ode to her favorite movie. I said that that was a good movie and that I actually was good friends with the producer's daughter when at university, that she lived in London now, that he had died when we were students, and I had had to console her. I said that movie was filmed at a prestigious Los Angeles hotel and that it's a great location for a film production. She said she had to go, so she went to the bathroom. I stayed on the terrace and smoked while she got herself in order. When she was ready to go, I naturally went inside. The timing just worked.

She was ready to go. I walked her to the door. She smiled. She gave me a kiss. Then I opened the door for her. Then she said, "See you next time." That smile. The eye contact. She left her speaker on the desk so I called out to her and she came back and got it. She appreciated this and it normalized the moment. I had thought of just letting it go but I didn't want to have to hold it until next time. It was big. After she left I freshened up and went to the Pinault Collection and then ate a lot of food and slept. It went perfect. It just got better and better as it went on. Infinite.

It was as if all my experience and training, programming, was a system. How the elements of the system relate, how likely or unlikely certain things are to be important. With the game changing as it's played. My long term structuring of myself, accounting for ongoing changes to the extent that I was able to, seemed to be moving the entire system, myself, towards the outcome I wanted. The leverage point, the bottleneck, was time, fate and chance.

I went back to Zürich because everything for my Oma was in order. St. Moritz was still available, but I didn't want to go back immediately. They had extended the chalet sojourn, and decided to record an album. Marcel on bass, he did know how to keep it steady.

I made an appearance at the office, and because the real estate magnate had paid in advance, I really had no deadline. I was the only American, and with the general apathy that I was displaying, that I didn't really care, there was no way they could let me go. My boss liked me, and he knew it was a matter of settling affairs that were colliding worlds in unexpected ways. Nevertheless, I stayed through the week's end, and worked hard. It set a tone, but I didn't know when I'd be back.

I took the silver Porsche Carrera 996 down A3 and was approaching Grisons. At the A13, towards the Tiefencastel, I exited. The road got narrower. I went through the Tunnel Passmal and the Tunnel Solis. Route 3 turned into Route 27. At Silvaplanersee, I sped up even though it got busier. I was excited to tell Marcel something of substance, and that I was in on the film. Emerging from the shadows. I went faster after the roundabout to get onto Route 27 and was on Via Aguagliöls by the Lej de Champfèr. I passed the helipad on Via San Gian and I was at 200 kilometers an hour. I let the gas pedal go by the tennis club and then pressed hard. The road curved left and I had penetrated town. I should have slowed down, I should have known better, but I didn't. At the end of the St. Moritzersee, there's a hard roundabout and a sharp turn up the hill into town. My tires dug deep and there were no police cars. I accelerated up the hill and around the long U curve as if I was at Monte Carlo. It was absurd but I felt invincible. I didn't care. But I didn't care because I was thinking about her. It was a different feeling. A live reason to not care. The Devil was in my bones but God was in my heart. I skidded a V-turn right from Via Serlas to Via Johannes Badrutt because I knew they were at the Carlton Hotel. They had rented the top floor and debauchery was guaranteed. Even if I didn't drink, the energy compelled me forward, faster, momentum. The final U-curve. There was a motorcyclist. Ducati Panigale, last year's model. Black. Anonymous rider. I hit him head on. He shattered the windshield. He took the turn hard and he took the collision harder.

He was dead. I wasn't. I shut off the engine. I got out and went to the rider. He was a corpse. Neck broken. Blood letting out of the helmet. The leather Dainese suit creasing mahogany. He wasn't in the shade, so I moved on to the side by the wall, so the sweat and the sun wouldn't bother me. I went back into the light to shut off his motorbike. Back in the shade, I lit up a cigarette and waited for the police. I stared at the dead rider. I knew I had destroyed the harmony of the day, the pastoral beauty of a sanctuary where I'd be happy. I flicked the cigarette at the rider and it rolled to his right boot. Then I lit another and another and flicked them at the same spot. The fourth cigarette I smoked, I stared at the motionless body, where the blood dripped onto the pavement. And it was like entering Hell with applause. The Devil killed the rider today. I just know it. And God didn't care. I was at the edge of the gun, and even though I had shut off the motor, I was still driving. I kept thinking about her. I thought that she was the best thing that ever happened to me.

XI

THE POLICE interviewed me at the station. I smoked because, well, I was quitting, for Freya, in Milan. With that future, I didn't care right now. The authorities responded promptly to the scene and attended to their analysis with detail. There were no witnesses. The assessment of the vehicle damages and skid marks, along with the weather conditions, which were clear, road design, which was blind, and adherence to traffic rules, seemed suspect. The Porsche and the Ducati were impounded for forensic analysis. Swiss Traffic Law holds drivers to a high standard of care, with strict liability applied even if the motorcyclist shared fault. I thought it was his fault. I told the investigator.

The motorcyclist was driving recklessly. This was indicated by the single skid marks ahead on the road, for me, or behind on the road for the dead rider. He had been performing wheelies and altogether disturbing the peace. There was a case opened to determine whether I, the driver, acted with negligence or recklessness. I suppose I was reckless but they'd never know. I called the office and they had an attorney tell me I would be subject to charges of negligent homicide, a less severe charge than manslaughter but still significant. The criminal penalties included steep fines, based on my income levels. My license would be temporarily suspended. If they deemed my negligence significant, I could face a conditional prison sentence, meaning no actual jail time unless further offenses were to occur. I'd probably have to pay civil compensation to the rider's family, even if fault was shared. Though insurance would cover it, my premiums would rise.

It was still early in the morning, so there was no media coverage. In any case, the authorities wanted to keep it quiet. There was an upcoming festival that afternoon and through the weekend, and they did not want to create more work for themselves. I cooperated, reiterated that I had adhered to speed limits and signaling, and corroborated that the motorcyclist appeared out of nowhere due to factors such as speeding and recklessness. These major contributing factors created an inevitable collision. I was sober and had no prior driving offenses.

The investigation was to be lengthy but eventual determination of shared fault was a certainty, according to the attorney. I'd be prepared to compensate the rider's family and suffer temporary driving restrictions. The long term reputational or psychological impact, I could worry about that later.

I reflected that I had killed a man. Vessel to vessel, machine to machine, life to life, an impact. It didn't make me feel altogether devastated, but it had happened. I couldn't deny fact. If I wasn't there, the rider would be alive. Fault did not matter. It was physics. Occupying space-time, at that position, and the outcome. No one hated me. No one punished me. The Swiss authorities acted on formalities. I met Marcel on the top floor of the Carlton and didn't mention it.

I was calm again. I was calm, in general, but my insides were back to the steady sedation of no meaning. An animal with stimuli. I fell asleep on a couch and when I woke up, it was night. The mountain peak had turned from a grass green to a cool blue under the moonlight. The silent luxury of the St. Moritz kept the pacing of the room steady. Muffled voices from the foyer. Civilized company. The reality of peace and no consequence. I wanted to thank God. I wanted to thank the Devil, too. Make sure to pay respects and shake the hands of any influence that may be involved. I felt pity for the rider's family but I didn't feel bad for the rider. He was in the wrong place at the wrong time. And he was riding a motorcycle. What did he expect was going to happen? A horse and a locomotive. Control the risk, control the environment. Man invented God's protection. I thought of Valeria and how she had died the same way. Even there, in St. Moritz, that next room with Hollywood and dreams, I drifted away and went back to family. My Oma, her arrangements, and how she had gifted me the world. We didn't even speak the same language. A guardian angel. The evening seemed to twist memory into opinion and as the images and sounds faded into the fog, all I had were impressions and feelings. I thought of Tokyo and how I'd take Freya there. I felt ready to live it all. As if the death of love, the acceptance of God and the recognition of the Devil gave me hope. What would happen would happen and it wasn't up to me. As if the strain of man was in vain, and if I considered myself a man, well, I was still an animal. As if my experience eviscerated the conscience, an untamed horse, wildfire inside, was now a heap of ash, cremated, entombed. A shrine of honor, a past housed in a book. No hope. I was open to the cruel pleasure of suffering and letting it be an experience that I'd conquer, overcome, and altogether, forget about. I had moved on. The world didn't care. The world was like me—a brutal rock, a constant force, something real that I could lean on—I felt alive and that I was alive, along the battle of life, on my isolated glacier. For there was a girl, now, and well, I may be dead inside, but she was alive, and I'd act the same, so we'd be equal. All I could wish for was the coming of Milan and for God and the Devil to greet me with claps of applause. For God and the Devil to let me go. To let me be. Dead and free. True life.

www.ingramcontent.com/pod-product-compliance
Lightning Source LLC
Chambersburg PA
CBHW051114300726
48981CB00002B/128